CASTING DOUBT

FISH CAMP COZY MYSTERIES, BOOK 2

SUMMER PRESCOTT

SUMMER PRESCOTT BOOKS PUBLISHING

Copyright 2025 Summer Prescott Books

All Rights Reserved. No part of this publication nor any of the information herein may be quoted from, nor reproduced, in any form, including but not limited to: printing, scanning, photocopying, or any other printed, digital, or audio formats, without prior express written consent of the copyright holder.

**This book is a work of fiction. Any similarities to persons, living or dead, places of business, or situations past or present, is completely unintentional.

CHAPTER ONE

Former Editorial Assistant and city girl, Eugenia Barkley, stared at the end of her fishing pole, wondering if she'd lost her mind. A cabin in the Ozarks had been bequeathed to her by her estranged mother, followed almost immediately by Eu being edged out of her job by an incompetent relative of her boss, and it had seemed as though fate had played a strange but compelling hand in deciding her future.

Eu's original plan had been to go to the Ozarks, get the cabin listed, sell it, and move on with her life. But once she discovered bits and pieces about the mother she never knew, that seemed to challenge all of her assumptions, she decided to stay long enough to find the truth about the woman who abandoned her.

So, there she sat, wrapped in layers of clothing, because she'd had no need for a winter coat in L.A, waiting for the delicate tap on the end of her pole that would signal the interest of a fish. The weather had turned from the pleasant temperatures of fall to the blustery beginnings of what seemed to indicate an oncoming winter that would challenge her patience and tax her resolve.

A large, sullen woman of indeterminate age, Crappie Callie – so named because she was a local legend when it came to catching Crappie – sat directly across the fishing hole from her, not even glancing in her direction. Eu had no idea what she'd done to earn the fisherwoman's wrath, but Callie had made it clear that she wanted nothing to do with the outsider from California.

Despite the chill in the air that became biting when the wind blew, Callie seemed perfectly fine sitting in her folding chair wearing only a plaid flannel shirt and ancient jeans with elastic at the waist.

"Hey, there," a cheery male voice called out.

Michael. Eu's heart skipped a beat. She'd developed quite a crush on the physics professor who spent his summers at a cabin a stone's throw away from hers.

He was at least six or seven years older than Eu, but had the looks, energy, and magnetism of a much younger man.

He appeared in the doorway of the structure that surrounded the large rectangular fishing hole that had been built into a dock, looking as handsome as ever.

"Any luck today?" he asked, glancing at Eu's pole and then Callie's.

Callie merely shrugged.

Eu smiled ruefully and shook her head. "Nope. It's a little scary. I have a nice stash of fish in my deep freeze, but I don't think it'll last more than a month or so."

"So, you're still planning to stay, huh?" Michael asked, his gaze grave.

"Yeah, for a while, at least. I think I'm going to give up for today though, and do a little grocery shopping," Eu replied, reeling in her line.

Just as she lifted her hook out of the water and threw her minnow into the lake as a snack for whatever might be below, Callie got a huge bite that nearly dipped the tip of her pole in the water. She glanced over at Eu and smirked as she battled whatever was on the end of the line.

Deflated, Eu leaned her pole against a cleaning table at the back of the structure and headed for the door. To her surprise and delight, Michael fell in step with her as she headed back up the hill toward her cabin.

"Do you need a ride to the grocery store?" he asked.

"I don't want to impose. I was just going to get an Uber," Eu replied.

"It's not an imposition at all. In fact, I'd be happy to help you strategically select some supplies that will help you get through the winter," Michael offered.

"That would be great, thanks."

"No problem. Do you know how to fish with jerkbait?" he asked.

Eu laughed. "Why does that sound like a trick question? Is that even a thing?"

Michael grinned. "Yes, it is. It's a manner of reeling in a lure that works particularly well in the winter months. I can show you how before I leave if you'd like."

Eu's smile faded a bit. "That would be nice. I forgot that you're only here through the season."

"Yeah, I've been working remotely for a few weeks, but it's time to get back and get in the classroom again."

"Duty calls, I guess."

"Indeed. I've stayed longer than I typically do already, so I'll be heading out soon. How about you? Any projections on how long you'll be here?" Michael asked.

"No idea. The more I find out about my mother, the more confused I get. So, until I find some sort of closure, I guess I'll be here." Eu shrugged.

"Brave." Michael nodded.

"Or nuts," Eu replied, her smile returning.

"Both?" he asked.

Eu laughed. "Probably."

Eu gazed out of her living room window at the grey sky and lake beyond and shivered, pulling a blanket over her legs as she curled up on the couch. Her phone rang, and the photo of a smiling face from home made her smile. "Hey, Fran," she answered, over the moon to hear from her best friend.

Fran wasted no time in getting to the point. Without so much as a greeting, she demanded to know when Eu would be coming back to L.A.

Eu sighed. "As much as I miss you and my old life there in the sunshine, I have some things to figure out and I'm just not ready to leave until I do. And I mean, honestly, I have no idea where life will take me after that."

There was a brief moment of silence as Fran processed. "Yeah, I get it. I just worry about you, and I hate the fact that you're going to be out there in the middle of nowhere alone in the winter," she said finally.

"I think I've done a good job of preparing. Michael took me shopping earlier and showed me a different way to fish for the winter," Eu reassured her.

"Lucky girl," Fran teased.

"Yeah, I'm not looking forward to him leaving, he's like my only friend here." Eu sobered, her stomach fluttering with worry.

"And I'm really not looking forward to you being there alone and so far from home," Fran replied.

"I'll be okay. There are just some things I have to figure out before I move on, you know?" Eu said, injecting confidence into her tone to ease Fran's mind a bit.

"Yeah, I get it. Just be careful, okay? And don't be afraid to change your mind and get out of there if you need to. There's been weird stuff happening to you from day one since you got there," Fran reminded her.

"I know. I'm leaving my options open. I can work from anywhere, and if I need to go, I'll go."

"Alright, bestie. Hang in there."

After hanging up, Eu immediately felt loneliness creeping in and she vowed to defeat it by keeping busy. She'd just finished an article for the online magazine who'd been sending her assignments, so since she had a bit of time on her hands, she decided to explore the cabin a bit more. It seemed as though every time she went looking for information about her mother in the cabin, something new and perplexing turned up.

Eu made a plan to start her exploration in the closets. She'd search every one of them top to bottom and then, if she didn't find anything, would move on to the outdoor shed attached to the porch wall, because in short order it would be too cold to do any outdoor searching.

"If I were someone who wanted to hide things, where would I hide them?" she mused, hands on hips, staring into the walk-in closet in the main bedroom. Gazing at the walls and floor, she moved slowly into the closet and noticed a pronounced creak when she stepped on a spot in the left hand corner, furthest away from the door. She shifted her weight from side to side and felt the floorboards give just a tiny bit.

"Well, maybe this is a good place to start."

She dropped down to her knees and started pressing on the floor close to the corner. When she pressed out from the corner, the floor seemed to give a bit for about two feet along each wall and about two feet out into the room, which would normally be covered by hanging clothing, but Eu only used a tiny fraction of the built in closet, because when she came to the Ozarks, she hadn't planned on staying long.

"I hate to mess up this amazing carpet." She ran her hand over the thick, velvety, cream-colored fibers. "But I guess it's mine to mess up, so I might as well try."

Eu grabbed hold of the fibers in the corner and tugged gently. To her surprise, the carpet gave way and came up easily. When she peeled the corner back, she noticed it was finished on the back side in a manner that would make it easy to set it back in place, making it look like it had never been touched.

Her heart thudded in her chest as she pulled on the corner of the carpet and revealed wooden planks like the ones throughout the main areas of the house. These planks, however, were shorter, each ending at a two-foot length that formed a perfect square.

"That's not something you see every day."

Eu leaned forward and tried to get her fingers between the outer plank and the one surrounding it, but was afraid to break her fingernails, so she hurried to the kitchen for something.

The moment she slipped the blade of the butterknife between the planks and tilted it; the planks rose up as one solid door.

"Whoa!" she gasped, pushing the carpet back further to open the door completely.

CHAPTER TWO

There were two wooden boxes, covered by some towels that matched the ones in the kitchen, and what looked like a painting, wrapped in brown paper, underneath the floorboards.

Eu took out the larger of the two boxes and opened it. Her heart ached when she saw what it contained.

"These are her paints," she murmured.

Eu had seen her mother's initials on a spectacular painting that graced one of the living room walls, and discovering this intimate part of her, tucked away beneath the floorboards made a lump rise in her throat. "She was an artist. I wasn't expecting that," she whispered, running her hands over the tubes of acrylic paint, brushes, and a well-used palette.

She moved the paints and brushes around to see if there were any hidden compartments in the wooden box, but when she didn't find any, she set it aside and took the smaller box out of the hidden space.

The smaller box contained a leather working kit with pieces of leather, various tools and templates. She picked up one of the templates and it looked familiar, but she couldn't quite place why. She ran a finger over the geometric patterns that had a native look to them and puzzled but couldn't figure out where she might have seen it before. Setting it back in the box, she carefully pulled out the paper-wrapped painting and lifted the tape that held the paper in place.

Feeling fragile, Eu pulled away the paper and saw a painting of a little girl, who looked to be no more than two, walking away, holding her daddy's hand and looking back over her shoulder, her eyes flooded with tears. She swallowed hard, then took a deep breath.

Checking the rest of the hidden space and finding nothing else, Eu put the two boxes back for the moment, then closed the small door and replaced the carpet. She took the painting and put it on top of her dresser, leaning against the wall. She stared at it for a moment, then shook herself out of her reverie.

"I'm assigning way too much meaning to this," she muttered. "She probably saw some kid with her dad at the playground while she was staying here."

Feeling far too emotional to be objective, she decided to stop searching and defaulted to her usual activity when she needed to think – fishing.

Her last minnow had met its watery end the day before, so Eu's first stop would have to be at the general store up the hill. A nice brisk walk that burned her calves and made her breathe harder would go a long way toward clearing her head.

"Hey. Trixie," she greeted the gravelly-voiced proprietor.

"How's it going, Eu?" Trixie replied, looking up from her fishing magazine.

"It's going." Eu shrugged. "I need some minnows when you have a chance," she said, holding up her Styrofoam bucket.

"Gotcha." Trixie set her magazine down on the counter and slipped down from her stool. "I'm closing up for the winter next week, you know."

"Yeah, I know. I'm going to miss being able to just walk up the hill for everything I need."

"It ain't none of my business, honey, but just how do you think you're gonna survive this winter with no one up here but you and Callie?" Trixie asked, dipping minnows into the bucket.

"Well, I've stocked up on supplies – Michael helped me – and he taught me how to fish with jerkbait and other baits so that I can still catch fish without minnows. I can work from here, so I should be all set."

Trixie quirked an eyebrow. "Mmhmm…" she grunted, clearly skeptical. "Well, I've learned that when people get their minds set on something, there ain't no use in trying to talk 'em out of it, so you do you, I guess. Just be careful. You ain't dumb, so you just might survive, I s'pose."

"Well, that's the goal." Eu smiled wryly.

"Since I'm closing things up, I got a whole bunch of perishable food I can give you, if you're interested.

Chips, candy, fruit, a few veggies, cereal…you can even put some of the milk in your deep freeze…" Trixie listed off items, gazing around the store.

"That would be great. The fewer times I have to Uber to the grocery store this winter, the better. Thank you, Trixie," Eu said, her heart warmed by the kindness behind the tough exterior.

"Don't mention it. There's also a couple of sweatshirts leftover from this season that I won't be able to sell next season because they got dates on 'em, so you can have them, too." She shook her head. "California girl coming to the Ozarks with no winter clothes."

"Oh, that'll be great. It's already getting chilly here in the mornings," Eu replied. "It'll take me quite a few trips for all the food, but I'll walk back and forth this afternoon, if that works for you."

Trixie waved a hand dismissively. "Nah. I'll just load up the Jeep and drive it down there to ya. I'll leave it on the porch, and you can put it away when you're done fishing."

"Oh, that'll really help. Thank you. Mind if I take a candy bar with me?" Eu grinned.

Trixie rolled her eyes. "They're all yours anyway, kiddo. Take whatever you want."

Munching on a candy bar, Eu made the trip back down to the cabin in a much happier mood, thankful for fresh air, sweet chocolate, and good people.

Callie wasn't at the fishing hole when Eu entered the shack with her bucket of minnows, which somehow made her feel stressed rather than relieved, but then again, not having to sit across from someone who refused to acknowledge her existence wouldn't be awful either.

Easing down into her camp chair and propping her feet up on the rail around the fishing hole after she dropped her line in the water, Eu exhaled, feeling the worries and stress starting to melt away. Nothing was quite as calming as watching the tip of her pole intently, waiting for a fish to take the bait. She'd learned at her dad's side, and the simple act of dropping her line in the water took her back to the sweet companionship they'd shared.

Eu's thoughts wandered, though she kept her eye on her pole. For a while, she watched a spider wrapping up its prey on a web, then she watched a regular pain-in-the-petunias visitor, a snapping turtle that she'd nicknamed Leonardo, after an irritating coworker, gliding around the perimeter of the fishing hole, trolling for stray minnows or other snacks.

"Go away, Leo," she said, when the turtle got a bit too close to her line. The last thing she wanted to deal with was unhooking a wayward turtle.

When Eu started wondering if she should bring a broom down to knock the cobwebs from the walls and ceiling, she realized something…there hadn't been any bites.

She reeled in her line and checked to see if she still had a minnow, or if some sneaky Drum fish might've taken it, but her minnow was still on. Which worried her. Were the fish going to stop biting this early in the season? She had a good stash but still wanted to increase her supply.

"Hey, there! Any bites?" she heard Michael ask.

Her heart jumped. She looked up and noticed that instead of his usual outdoor gear, he was wearing nicer jeans and a button-down shirt. It was a good look for him, and he definitely looked more like a professor.

"Not so far, no."

"Well, don't worry about it. Things tend to slow down this time of year, but they're still out there waiting to be caught," Michael said, his confident smile warming her from head to toe.

"I hope so. You look nice today," she blurted, suddenly hyper-aware of her baggy sweatshirt and worn capris. She had flip-flops on for goodness' sake. She felt a flush rising in her cheeks and hoped that he didn't notice it.

"Thanks. Yeah, it's time to get back to the real world." He shrugged.

"Oh." Eu's stomach dropped. "When are you leaving?"

"Today. I'm all packed, finally. How are you holding up? Find out anything else about your mom?" he asked. Eu knew that she'd miss the way his brow furrowed slightly when he was discussing a serious topic.

"Yeah, I didn't realize how important her art was to her, but I found a secret stash of her painting and leather working supplies. I guess no one is as one dimensional as I've always believed her to be." She swallowed against the lump in her throat.

"That's an important insight, Eugenia," Michael said quietly. Her heart leapt at the sound of her name. Somehow it didn't sound horribly old-fashioned and stuffy when he said it. "Hopefully you'll see an even bigger picture as you discover more."

Eu nodded. "I hope so."

Michael glanced at his watch. "I'd better head back up now, my Uber will be here any minute."

Eu frowned, her stomach doing a little flip. "Your Uber? Is something wrong with your car?"

Michael smiled, shaking his head. "No. I'm just thinking that you'll need it here much more than I need it back home. I have other means of transportation." He dug into his pocket and handed her his keys.

"Oh. That's so sweet, but no. I couldn't impose upon you like that." Eu held the keys out to him, but he ignored them.

"It's for the sake of my students," he said.

"Huh? Your students? What do you mean?"

"If I leave, knowing that you have no transportation other than spending a million dollars to take an Uber to the grocery store, I wouldn't be able to concentrate," he teased kindly. "Seriously though, I don't need the car back home, and my Uber should be arriving any second. I have to go." He opened his arms, and Eu went into them without another thought. His hug was warm and entirely appropriate. Eu knew she'd be wondering if it affected him the way it affected her all winter, and she was more than okay with it.

"Take care of yourself, Eu. Here's my email and phone number if you need anything. Don't hesitate to use them," he said, producing a business card with his cell number written on the back.

"Thank you, Michael. I don't know what I would have done without your kindness," Eu replied, trying to keep her voice from shaking.

"And now you won't have to find out." With another grin, he went out the door, and Eu watched him, waving when he turned around at the top of the hill. Somehow, the breeze felt chillier, and the resort felt empty. Eu reeled in her line and tossed her minnow to Leo the turtle, then trudged up the hill. The curtains at Michael's windows were drawn and she shivered, unconsciously rubbing her upper arms.

When she got to her porch, there was a giant basket waiting for her, along with coolers and sacks full of groceries from the general store. The basket was covered with a red and white checked cloth and smelled heavenly. It was loaded with bread and other baked goods that Michael had prepared. There was a note attached.

You don't have to eat it all at once, all of this freezes, but the brownies are still warm if you're hungry. It should last most of the way through the winter. Enjoy.

CHAPTER THREE

Michael had been the last of the seasonal owners to leave the resort, and life had taken on an eerie cast in his absence. The parking lot was empty and there were no sounds of simple things like children playing on the playground, cars coming and going, and the talking and laughter of fishermen making their way to their boats or docks.

Eu had been working hard at writing articles every day to try and build a stockpile of money for the inevitable time when she would choose to leave the Ozarks and start a new life. Fishing during the morning and working in the afternoons and evenings had become her routine, and while it was solitary, she felt accomplished somehow.

When Eu went shopping with Michael, she'd stocked up on different baits to try when her minnows ran out. She pushed three tiny sparkly pink marshmallows that smelled like sun-dried fish onto her hook and dropped it into the water, hoping it might break the slump she'd been in. She'd only caught two fish over the past week.

Hopeful, but not confident, she lowered her diva hook into the water and waited. Callie, whom she'd greeted every day, to no avail, had rolled her eyes when Eu brought out her brightly colored bait.

Since things had been so slow, Eu poured herself a cup of coffee from her thermos, thinking she'd have plenty of time to drink it before getting a bite, but the tip of her pole bounced so hard she sloshed hot coffee over her hand in her haste to put it down next to her chair.

She set the hook and reeled hard. Whatever was on the end of her line, it was fighting like crazy. She grinned fiercely and struggled to keep the tip of her rod up the way her father had taught her to do. Something huge broke the surface and tried to dive down again, but Eu battled it like a trooper, reaching behind her chair for the large net that she'd purchased soon after arriving in the Ozarks.

She held the line, with the large fish swimming just below the surface, and maneuvered the net beneath it, scooping it up. It was too heavy to lift with just one hand, so she set her pole on the dock and hefted it up with both hands, seeing a massive catfish. She brought him up and over the rail that surrounded the fishing hole and set him, still in the net, on the dock.

There was a huge amount of meat on the catfish, but she stared down at it perplexed. She had no idea how to even pick it up safely, without her hands falling victim to its barbs, much less how to clean it.

"Wow, that's a beauty!" Eu heard. She looked up and saw a tanned man with a blonde crewcut who looked like he was around the same age as Michael. He had apparently just finished tying up his boat at the closest dock on the marina. He trotted over to come see the fish.

"Thanks. I wish I knew what to do with it. I don't even know how to pick it up to take it off the hook," Eu admitted.

Seeming like someone who didn't spend much time in fishing holes, the man, who smelled of expensive cologne, laughed.

"No worries, it's easy to do and I'd be happy to show you, but I need to go run and get some things from my boat."

"Oh, really? That would be amazing, thank you!" Eu breathed a sigh of relief.

He was back in a flash, with a bright yellow and black glove and a knife that glimmered in the sun.

He handed her the glove and explained how to pick up the catfish safely. She did as he suggested and took the hook out of the giant's mouth. Together they went to the cleaning station, Eu's arm aching from the weight of the beast, and he walked her step by step through the cleaning and fileting process.

"See? Easy peasy. You did a great job and now you have some beautiful filets," the man said. "You can keep the glove. I've got a bunch of 'em at home and I don't get out to fish nearly as much as I'd like anyway."

"Do you live here in the resort?" Eu asked.

"Nah, I just stop here sometimes to get bait or a snack. You see that white house with the pillars across the way, on the bluff?"

Eu squinted in the direction that he was pointing and put her hand over her eyes to block the sun. "You mean the one up at the top with the flagpole?" she asked.

"Yep. That's my house. Are you local?"

"Well, sort of. I'm living in the resort through the winter, but I doubt it'll be my permanent situation," Eu replied.

"Wow. That's a gutsy move, especially if you're not familiar with lake life. Good for you, but if I were you, I wouldn't share that information with too many folks," he advised.

Before Eu could ask what he meant, he reached for his wallet and produced a business card.

"This is me. If you need anything, I can probably get here quicker than emergency services, so just give me a jingle," he said, handing it to her.

"Benz Zoeller," she read aloud. "Well, it's nice to meet you, Benz Zoeller, and thank you for the catfish lesson."

"You're more than welcome. Take care now," he said, giving her a jaunty wave as he left the fishing hole.

Callie had disappeared when Benz was showing Eu how to filet, leaving Eu alone with her thoughts.

"Well, I've got some hefty filets that I need to get into the freezer, so I guess I'm done for today," she said with a smile.

It had been nice meeting Benz. He was easy to talk to and seemed so knowledgeable that she wouldn't hesitate to text him with a question if necessary. Thankful to have met a kind local, she headed back to the cabin.

Her filets stashed in the freezer; Eu sat down on the couch with her laptop to work on her latest article: Ten Ways to Know That He's the One. Though no one was there to see her, she blushed when Michael immediately popped up in her mind. She was deep into her research when Fran called to check on her.

"That article is about Michael isn't it?" Fran teased.

"Stop it!" Eu protested. "It's odd though. All the research I've found points out certain traits..." she began.

"And let me guess...he meets every one of them," Fran interrupted.

"Well, I mean...yeah. He definitely does. But he'd never be interested in someone like me."

"Oh puhleeze," Fran drawled. "He probably has a secret crush on you."

"Yeah, right. Whatever. So, tell me what's going on with you." Eu abruptly changed the subject.

Fran clearly noticed, but didn't say anything about it, instead launching into a story about a surfer customer that she had that sent Eu into gales of laughter. It was just the boost she needed.

Talking with Fran had lightened her mood considerably and when Eu looked out and saw a breathtakingly beautiful golden light shimmering on the lake, turning the trees with their autumn leaves into a riot of color, she had a sudden carefree impulse to paint.

Hurrying to the secret space in the closet, she retrieved her mother's painting set, hoping the paint tubes inside were still usable. When she opened the box, the thought struck her that the towels her mother used to clean her brushes were the same kind of towels that were in the kitchen. Her mother had obviously cleaned her own brushes. Had she cleaned the cabin, too? Had she done laundry? Dishes? Because none of that computed with the picture of her that Eu had formed in her head over the years.

The paints were still in excellent condition, and when Eu picked up the first brush, her breath caught. Her mother's hands had held that brush. They'd never held her hand, even as a little girl, but they'd held the brush… and had made magic happen.

Her eyes welling with tears, Eu squeezed out a blob of blue and a blob of white to make the clearest of blue skies. Her strokes were tentative at first, but it soon seemed that her mother had passed more down to her than a cozy cabin. After painting the backdrop of an autumn sky, Eu decided to let it dry before continuing to work on the painting.

She thoroughly rinsed her brush, standing at the sink and feeling an odd kinship to the woman who had stood there before her. Watching the color flow out of the brush under the stream from the faucet was surprisingly relaxing. The thought that her mother had enjoyed such simple pleasures was hard to wrap her head around.

Shaking off a feeling that she couldn't quite place, Eu stashed the painting set back in its proper place and decided to do a bit of cleaning in the cabin. She dusted anything that needed it, then grabbed the vacuum and started vacuuming in her bedroom.

Trying to be as thorough as possible and wanting to take good care of the largest thing she'd ever owned; Eu bent down and made the vacuum cleaner go flat so that she could reach as far under the bed as possible. She hadn't reached very far when the vacuum made a loud clanking noise, like someone was tapping a fork against the roller. She hit the off switch and got down on her knees to peer under the bed. A glint of metal caught her eye and when she reached for it and brought it out, it was a small key. It had initials on it that meant nothing to her – NBO – and a three-digit number – 017.

"Where did this come from?" she wondered, checking out the key, then pocketing it before using her cell phone to examine the underside of the bed. She found nothing of interest, and when she stood back up to restart the vacuum, the tranquil quiet of the nearly empty resort was shattered by the scream of multiple sirens, their lights painting Eu's foyer and living room in red and blue.

"Oh, geez. What now?" Eu sighed, leaving the vacuum in place and hurrying to the foyer to peer out at the flood of law enforcement and rescue vehicles streaming into the parking lot.

Slipping her feet into a pair of well-worn running shoes and tossing on one of the hoodies that Trixie donated to her, Eu headed out once the sirens stopped.

Deputies, state police, the fire department, and disturbingly, a coroner's van had filled the resort parking lot on the side near the fishing hole, and personnel were hurrying toward the marina.

"Oh, no." Eu's heart rate accelerated, and she felt sick to her stomach. "I hope Callie is okay."

As she jogged down the cement walkway that led to the marina and the fishing hole, she was relieved to see a very pale Callie heading up the hill toward her.

"Oh, it's good to see, you," Eu said, a bit breathless. "Are you okay?"

Callie, as was her custom, merely glared at her and brushed past without a word. She was carrying her tackle box and Eu noticed she wore a leather bracelet on her right wrist.

"Well, I guess it's good to know that some things never change," Eu muttered, continuing down toward the fishing hole.

Her heart sank when she saw deputies Carter and Writman heading up the walkway toward her.

"Good morning, Deputies," she said tonelessly, planning to brush by them as Callie had brushed by her.

"We need to ask you a few questions," Carter replied grimly, both of them ignoring her greeting.

"What a shock," Eu replied dryly. "What's going on anyway? Can I just go down there and grab my thermos?"

"No, ma'am," Carter said, as Writman shifted to the side to block the sidewalk like she was going to try and bulldoze her way through. "There's an active investigation going on and the area is cordoned off."

"Are Callie and I in danger here?" she asked, as two techs from the coroner's office carried a folded gurney down the hill.

Before Carter could answer, Writman decided to weigh in.

"Where were you last night between seven o'clock and five a.m. this morning?" he demanded, gazing at her as though she was a hardened criminal.

"Seriously? We're doing this again?" Eu's brows rose and she shook her head in disbelief.

"We need to establish if you saw or heard anything," Carter interjected.

"No, I didn't. Last night at seven o'clock, I was doing what I always do – working on my computer. I went to bed around ten, like I always do, and you can bet your buttons that at five a.m. I was sound asleep like most normal humans."

"I was up at five a.m.," Writman said.

"Case in point," Eu rolled her eyes.

"Look, we're investigating a possible homicide here, so if there's anything you remember seeing or hearing that was out of the ordinary in the past few days, just let us know, okay?" Carter said, before Writman could think of a retort.

"A homicide?" Eu's stomach churned.

"Yeah, and we've got our eye on you," Writman replied. "Seems like the murder rate has really picked up since you came to town."

"Then once again, you're barking up the wrong tree and giving an actual criminal time to get away. Good luck with your investigation," Eu said. She shivered and dug her hands deeply into her pockets, turning to leave.

CHAPTER FOUR

It didn't take long for Eu to discover the barest of details of the homicide. When she did a search, it was all over Ozark news sources. The victim of the suspected homicide was a local celebrity of sorts, a wedding DJ, Raz Wiles. His body had been found in the water near a dock in the marina. When Eu read the name of the company that Raz worked for, she recognized it immediately, because it had been on a list of companies on the card that Benz Zoeller had given her, which sent a bit of a shiver up her spine. It was an odd coincidence, and if she hadn't seen how nice Benz was, in person, she might wonder about him.

With no further details given about the circumstances of the death, Eu had no choice but to follow the one possible lead the news had provided. It was definitely time to contact Benz Zoeller.

Settling in on her couch, she took a deep breath and dialed his number. He picked up on the first ring, and Eu reintroduced herself.

"Of course I remember," Benz said, sounding glad to hear from her. "Did you cook up those big filets yet?" He chuckled.

"No, not yet. I'm saving them for when I'm really hungry," Eu replied, put at ease by his friendly manner.

"Understandable. How are you doing? Did you need help with something?" he asked.

"No, I'm fine, thanks. Actually, I was just calling to see how you're doing. There was quite an event here at the marina yesterday, and I saw online that one of your employees had passed. That has to be an awful feeling," Eu said.

There was a silence on the other end of the line that made her think she'd overstepped.

"I'm sorry, it's none of my business. I was just hoping that you were doing okay," she blurted.

"No, I totally appreciate that, thank you," Benz replied, his tone quiet but not negative. "Yeah, it was such a senseless tragedy. Raz was young and had a bright future ahead of him."

"It's so sad that he might have been murdered," Eu said. "I've always wondered how someone could kill another person. It's so beyond horrifying."

"Yeah, it takes a special kind of psycho, I guess," Benz replied. "But Raz didn't live an entirely innocent life either. He was a shameless ladies' man and that could definitely have gotten him into a sticky situation. I also recently had some really negative reports about him from some couples who he'd DJ'd for, and who knows what might have happened with that. Is an unsatisfactory reception a motive for murder? Your guess is as good as mine, but I'm sure the police have their hands full with the potential suspects in the area."

Eu replied with appropriately sympathetic platitudes. They chatted a bit about fishing and then ended the call, leaving her curious and ready to explore the tidbits of info she'd gotten from Benz.

Grabbing her laptop, she pulled up the society pages from the local paper to look for mentions of the DJ, or pictures where he was in the background of recent weddings. She spotted one photo where the bride was glaring toward the stage at her reception, arms crossed, as many of the rest of the guests stared at her. Eu found her name in the short article beneath the photo, which just talked about how radiant she looked and how the wedding had been something out of a fairytale.

Determined to find Raz's killer so that Carter and Writman would leave her alone once and for all, Eu concocted a plan.

"Okay then, Murphy Miche…you and I are going to have a little chat."

Another quick search turned up the bride's address, and before she could change her mind, Eu grabbed the keys that Michael had given her and walked down to his cabin to get the car he'd left for her. The spotless sedan smelled faintly of a combination of his cologne and buttery soft leather seats.

Eu put her seat belt on and sat in the car for a moment, feeling silly that she was missing the presence of a man whom she'd known for about twenty seconds.

"Alright, Michael... I'll try to keep your car safe, I promise," she murmured, her stomach turning at the thought of something happening to it in his absence.

Her resolve strong, she put the key in the ignition and turned the engine over. The car drove like a dream, and in no time at all, she was pulling up to a large contemporary house near the lake.

She gathered up the notebook and pen that she'd brought with her, marched to Murphy Miche's door, and rang the bell.

A tall curvy blonde, with heavy makeup and the longest hair and eyelashes that Eu had ever seen – quite a feat for someone from L.A. – answered the door wearing a bubblegum pink velour track suit. She gave Eu a onceover and said, "Are you lost or something? I'm not buying anything."

Eu smiled. "I'm not selling anything, and I'm not lost. I'm a customer service agent from Dream Maker Enterprises, and I wanted to just express how profoundly sorry I am that you had a less than satisfactory experience. I'm hoping you'll provide some details about what went wrong at your reception."

"What went wrong? Are you kidding me? That loser DJ ruined everything. His timing on the first dance left everyone waiting for the music to begin, and he started playing this ridiculous song that I didn't even select during the cutting of the cake, which totally ruined the video. I could go on for days about all the mistakes he made."

Murphy ticked off the incidents on her fingers which sported nails that were painted a sparkly hot pink and were so long that Eu wondered how she functioned in life. She made it obvious that she was listening intently and sympathetically and jotted down notes in an effort to look more official.

"I mean, I had planned on picking another company to DJ the reception, but my best friend recommended that Raz dude because he'd done her wedding. I didn't go to it because I was in Bora Bora at the time, so I trusted her judgment and hired him. Big mistake. Big. Huge." She gestured dramatically, her nails glinting in the sunlight.

"I am so sorry about that," Eu said, and Murphy spoke before she could continue.

"Yeah, and I'm so sorry that your company didn't give me any of my money back, even though I complained more than once," she shot back.

"I understand how that would be frustrating," Eu began, realizing that she was speaking with an obvious bridezilla. "That's not my decision, but I'll be sure to make a strong recommendation on your behalf. You mentioned your referral from your best friend…can you refresh my memory, what was her name again?"

Murphy's eyes narrowed. "You're the customer service rep and you don't have that information?"

Eu's heart leapt to her throat as her ruse threatened to derail, but she managed to control her reaction so that it didn't show. "Of course we have it in the file, but I don't happen to recall it at the moment. If you can just tell me again so that I can jot it down in my notes, I'll have it handy when I fill out my report."

Murphy pursed her lips but evidently bought Eu's story. "Lexie. Lexie Rouse."

Eu nearly wilted with relief but hid it by writing down the name. "Great, thanks. Is there anything else you'd like to add? I don't want to take up too much of your time."

"Yeah. I'd like to add that Raz Wiles should be fired. If he can't perform his one job, he doesn't deserve to have it."

Before Eu could reply, Murphy stepped back and slammed the door shut.

"Alrighty then," she muttered.

Her stomach growled as she sank back down into the comfy warmth of the driver's seat, and Eu realized that her next task would be whipping up something delicious for lunch. If she was going to approach the bridezilla's best friend, she wasn't going to do it on an empty stomach.

Thanks to Trixie's generosity and Michael's compulsion to bake, there were plenty of options to choose from for lunch. Eu wanted to use the fresh vegetables from the general store first, so she made a fantastic salad, adding leftover shredded chicken, then tossing it with her homemade dressing, and pairing it with two of Michael's homemade bread sticks.

While she munched, Eu searched for Lexie Rouse's home address and found it easily enough. Thankfully,

Murphy had provided her bestie's married name, which made the search much easier.

Fueled with a good lunch and her earlier success, Eu had no qualms about heading out to talk to Lexie Rouse. She was choosing to think of interviewing potential suspects as work experience that would at least give her the option of pursuing full-time reporting if she chose to in the future. Right now, her future goals and dreams had to be set aside while she worked to solve a crime and show local law enforcement that she wasn't a criminal.

Lexie lived in a neighborhood that was nice, but not as grand as Murphy's had been, and her traditionally styled home was about half the size of her bestie's. Eu used the same introductory story with Lexie that she had with Murphy, but it was received in a much more gracious manner.

"Yeah, Raz didn't do a perfect job at our wedding either, but I'm not nearly as obsessed with perfection as Murph is." Lexie smiled. "I mean, Raz was so captivating that I didn't care what he did, as long as he flashed his perfect teeth and cute little dimples when I talked to him."

"Are you two friends?" Eu asked, wondering how on earth neither Lexie nor Murphy had heard about the DJ's demise. But then again, she wouldn't have known if it hadn't happened practically on her doorstep, and she then went searching for info about it.

"Me and Raz? That's a tough one. He was so adorable." Lexie leaned forward a bit, glancing up and down the street as if spies might be out and about, hanging on their every word. "Just between us girls, Raz and I actually had a brief affair after the wedding. I know that probably sounds awful to you, and I suppose on some level it is, but, well, my husband, Nate, travels a lot. I know that may not sound like the greatest excuse, but he's also, well, I mean, he's an accountant, you know? He has a wicked temper when things don't go perfectly the way he expects them to. He's supposed to be home now, but his latest business trip got extended by a few days, so who knows when he'll be back and what kind of mood he'll be in." Lexie sighed. "You must think I'm a terrible person," she said.

"No, not at all. We love who we love, and sometimes there's an ebb and flow that can't be helped." Eu shrugged, trying desperately not to blush as Michael's face popped into her mind.

"Yeah, I feel that." Lexie nodded. "Anyway, I had been planning to tell Raz that he needed to do a really good job for Murph, because she's a social media influencer and she could get him a ton of new business, but then, I was afraid if I talked to him again, Nate might find out and go ballistic, so I just hoped for the best. Murph lost her mind because he wasn't on his game that night. I personally don't see why it was such a big deal for her, but she's a perfectionist, too, I guess. Maybe I'm just like, drawn to those kind of people," she mused.

Eu nodded, realizing that Lexie might just talk to her all day if given the chance, but it didn't seem like she had any more relevant info, so after chatting politely for a few more minutes, she left, thanking her for her time.

The light breeze gave her a chill as she walked back to the car, but once inside, she enjoyed the gorgeous fall colors that had blanketed the hills around the lake, slowing down to watch when a deer bounded across the road in front of her.

Back at the cabin, the first thing Eu did after setting down her purse and keys on the table in the foyer, was to go directly to the gas fireplace, using the remote control to turn it on low. She'd be doing some research on Murphy, Lexie, and Nate momentarily, and she wanted to be cozy warm while she did it.

Once she settled into her favorite spot on the couch where she could see the lake, the fireplace, and the TV, she tucked her feet up under her and opened her laptop. She'd barely looked at the results of her search for info about Murphy when a little chat box opened up on her screen.

It was Michael, and Eu was glad he wasn't there in person to hear her delighted intake of breath.

Hey Eu! How's life there? Saw there was a possible homicide at the resort. You okay?

Eu read his message and typed back.

Yep, I'm good. They'd love to blame me, AGAIN, but I'm trying to get ahead of it this time. I've already talked to two brides who might have a motive.

Eu watched three little dots light up in the chat box that meant Michael was typing.

Sounds risky. Anybody I know?

Maybe? The brides are Murphy Miche and Lexie Rouse. Lexie's husband's name is Nate, but I don't know who Murphy's husband is yet.

Yeah, you might want to stay out of this one. Nate Rouse is known for being a less than pleasant person. I've met him once or twice and he's bad news.

I wish I could stay out of it, but unfortunately, I'm sick of being suspicious somehow, just because I wasn't born here. I'm sorry, that sounded way bitter.

Not at all. Just be careful. I don't want to keep you, just thought I'd check in and see how you were doing. Have a great evening and don't hesitate to reach out.

Thanks. Great talking to you, Michael!

You too, Eugenia

Michael signed off and, gripped by a bout of loneliness, Eu closed her laptop, went to the refrigerator, took out a cinnamon roll, and warmed it up in the microwave. She relished the soft sweetness of it while she watched a rerun of Little House on the Prairie. Distracted by thoughts of eating cinnamon rolls on

Michael's porch, or at the fishing hole, she turned the TV off when the episode was over and headed for bed.

Tomorrow was another day, and she had investigating to do.

CHAPTER FIVE

After a couple of cups of coffee to shake the cobwebs from her brain, Eu headed down to the fishing hole. When she entered the shack built around the fishing hole, she looked through the opposite door and saw the remnants of police tape fluttering from the dock, not too far from where Benz had been when he showed her how to clean the catfish.

A woman stood on the dock, staring out over the lake, her arms wrapped around her midsection.

Eu set down her bucket with just a few minnows remaining in it and went over to the woman, not bothering to greet Callie, who hadn't even glanced up when she entered.

"Hey, there," she called out quietly as she approached. "Are you okay?"

She was slender with long auburn hair and when she turned, Eu saw they were about the same age and that the woman had a sprinkle of freckles across the bridge of her nose. She looked pale, and there were bags under her eyes as though she hadn't slept in a while.

"That's a hard question these days," she replied dully, seeming to hug herself a bit tighter. "I don't know if you heard about what happened here." She gestured to the dock and the water in front of it.

Eu nodded. "Yeah, I heard."

"Well, the man who was found. He was…" The woman stopped and took a deep breath. "He was my boyfriend."

"Oh, no. I'm so sorry. I can't even imagine how that must feel," Eu said gently. "I'm Eugenia, but people call me Eu. Do you want to talk about it?"

"Nice to meet you. I'm Sierra." It looked like she was trying to smile but couldn't quite pull it off. "I can't believe this happened. Raz was so talented and such a great guy." She shook her head and stared out at the lake again before continuing. "There was no reason for him to be anywhere near here." She turned to glance at Eu. "Did you ever meet him?"

"No. I'm new here, so I haven't met very many people. I live just right up the hill if you'd like to come up and have some coffee," Eu offered, her heart going out to the miserable soul in front of her.

"I'm afraid I can't right now, but thank you for the invitation," Sierra said, brushing away a tear. She turned back to the water.

"Do you have any idea how it might have happened?" Eu asked, feeling that maybe talking about the incident might help Sierra process her grief.

"He had two bad wedding clients in a row. One was a bridezilla who tried to trash his reputation on the internet, and the other was a groom with a really bad temper. Between the two of them, poor Raz got all kinds of hostile emails, phone calls in the middle of the night. It was ridiculous. His boss was jealous of him too, now that I think of it. His ex-wife flirted with Raz at a wedding and after that Zoeller gave him the worst gigs and refused to give him a promotion, or even a raise. I mean, I get it, I guess. Raz was younger, more attractive. I can see how Zoeller might be intimidated, but Raz was nothing but kind to everyone. Aside from drama from his job, he definitely didn't have any enemies." Sierra shrugged, her lower lip trembling.

Eu wondered if she'd heard about Raz's reputation as a ladies' man but kept the question to herself.

"I'm so sorry this happened to you," she said instead.

"I don't know why I came down here," Sierra said. "I guess I just wanted to see where he was found. Thank you for being so nice to me."

"I'm down here nearly every morning to fish, so if you want to hang out and talk or whatever, you're more than welcome to. Have the police talked to you about everything?" Eu asked.

Sierra nodded. "Yeah, they've been wonderful. Very thorough. I'm hoping they find whoever did this quickly so I can have some closure."

"I'm sure they will."

"Thanks for letting me vent," Sierra said.

"Anytime. Take care now," Eu said, turning to head back to the fishing hole.

"You, too," Sierra replied, her voice quavering.

Eu's heart was heavy as she went to her favorite spot by the fishing hole. Until now, her only thoughts regarding the murder had been about investigating to save her own skin. It meant more now that she realized there were people grieving the victim.

She entered the shack determined to be a better person who didn't just think about herself. Her resolve faltered a bit when she encountered resistance from Callie, however.

"Hi, Callie," she called out, determined to flood the dour woman with so much positivity that she'd eventually have to come around.

Callie's eyes didn't move from the tip of her pole.

"My friend Fran tells me you're a nice person, and I trust her judgement, so I'm going to keep being nice to you until you figure out that I'm not a bad person, despite whatever it is that my mother might have done."

Callie grimaced and rolled her eyes, but still stayed mute, not making eye contact.

"Look, we're the only ones who are going to be at the resort through the winter, so we should at least be on speaking terms," Eu tried again.

Eerily, Callie turned an icy gaze toward Eu. "You ain't gonna make it."

Icy fingers clutched at Eu's heart, but she was determined to stay positive. At least she'd gotten a response.

"Is that a threat?" she said, trying for a playful tone that seemed to fall unbearably flat.

Callie merely made a face at her and returned her gaze to her pole.

After a while of fishing in silence, with almost no luck aside from a few nibbles, Eu headed back up to the cabin to make her lunch and work on another article. The current one that she'd been contracted for was about toxic relationships and how to recognize them. As she trudged empty-handed back up the hill to the cabin, she muttered that Callie would be her inspiration if not her star subject.

CHAPTER SIX

Because Eu found the process of preparing food to be relaxing, she decided to fix a special lunch for herself. She needed comfort food and one of her favorite dishes was gnocchi, so she peeled and boiled some potatoes, getting out the flour and other ingredients while the pan of potatoes bubbled on the stove.

She brought out the dried herbs that she'd bought at Michael's suggestion when they'd made their last trip to the grocery store to stock Eu up for the winter. Grabbing butter, cream, and olive oil, she added the herbs, crushed garlic, and a dash of salt and pepper to make a simple sauce for her gnocchi. The kitchen smelled heavenly, and Eu was able to think about how she wanted to approach her latest article as she went through the various steps to pull together a lunch that would fill her belly and soul. As always, she made a small salad out of fresh greens, tomatoes, herbs, and onion to eat before her main meal, planning her article as she munched.

She'd made enough gnocchi to last for the next two or three days, so she'd use it as a side dish with other meals as a special treat.

The dish turned out exactly how she had hoped it would. The gnocchi were tender and delicious and the buttery sauce was decadent.

After her meal, which she deliberately kept small so that she wouldn't get sleepy, Eu put the leftovers away, loaded the dishwasher, and snuggled into the couch with her laptop.

Her intentions were good. She had planned out how she was going to write her latest article, but as she zoomed around the internet doing research, her mind kept returning to what Lexie Rouse and Michael had said about Nate Rouse. He seemed, from what she'd heard, like he'd be a good suspect, and he certainly had motive if he'd found out about his wife's dalliance with the handsome DJ.

Knowing she should be working instead of sleuthing; she tapped Nate Rouse's name into her search bar anyway and discovered that he'd been detained and/or arrested multiple times for aggressive or combative behavior. Odd for an accountant.

Eu chewed her bottom lip, trying to decide her next move.

"I need to talk to him. If I go to his work, he's probably less likely to get belligerent if he picks up on the fact that I'm trying to get information from him. I should stay here and write my article. I really should…"

Closing her laptop, Eu tapped her fingers on the top of it, thinking. He was dangerous, that was a fact, and he could be a killer. But he was also the most likely suspect. She should leave him alone and not 'poke the bear.'

But she wasn't going to. Not a chance.

She set her laptop aside and headed for the foyer, slipping on her shoes and grabbing her keys and purse, then stopped, her hand on the doorknob.

"Lexie said he was out of town. I don't want to waste a trip if he's not even in the office."

She looked up his office number on her phone and called it. When the receptionist answered, she asked to speak with Nate and was told that he was out of town and wouldn't be back for a couple days. After thanking the young man and hanging up, Eu couldn't help but wonder if Nate was staying away so that he could lay low until the case cooled off a bit.

"I'm definitely going to his office when he gets back," she vowed, putting her keys and purse back on the foyer table. She slipped off her shoes and turned to go back to the living room when a loud knock on the door made her jump, her heart skipping a beat.

"Oh, geez," she gasped, shaking her head.

When she opened the door and saw Carter and Writman standing on her porch yet again, she let out a sigh.

"Do you guys just like to pop over here when you get bored or something? Should I start stocking your favorite snacks in my pantry?" she asked.

"We have reports that you stopped by the residences of Murphy Miche and Lexie Rouse, under the guise of working as a customer service representative for Dream Maker Enterprises. We discovered it when we spoke to both of those ladies, and they said that a rep had finally stopped by. Video from their doorbells confirms that it was you," Carter said.

"What do you have to say for yourself?" Writman added.

"What do I have to say for myself?" Eu bristled, fed up. "I think it's utterly ridiculous that every time something weird happens nearby, I'm automatically a suspect or person of interest, or whatever, just because I'm new here. If all you're doing is trying to point fingers at me, I'm darn sure going to do some digging to prove you wrong. Who wouldn't? I mean seriously, the person responsible needs to be held accountable, but the victim's girlfriend needs some closure as well. How would you like to be worrying and wonder?" she asked, hands on hips, chest heaving with anger.

Carter's brows rose and he exchanged a glance with his partner. "Girlfriend? What girlfriend?"

Eu winced internally, wishing she hadn't just blurted that out. She'd figured they knew about Sierra since she'd said they'd been very kind and thorough, but she must have spoken to different deputies, or maybe the state police.

"I ran into her down at the dock. She was grieving and came to see the place where her boyfriend had been found." Eu shrugged.

"Name?" Writman barked.

"Umm. It was like Sara or something," Eu replied. It was technically true. The name Sierra was like Sara. Sort of. If it was in a sheriff's report somewhere, they'd find it.

"The fact that we keep hearing your name over and over in relation to this case only makes you look more suspicious," Writman accused.

"You need to know we're doing everything we can to solve this case and you need to back away before your involvement becomes interference," Carter interjected, before his partner could go into a tirade.

"Look, I get it, but my freedom is on the line here," Eu said, addressing Carter only. "I think I may be more motivated to find the correct person than some people are." She shot Writman a glare.

"You ever hear of obstruction? Because that's a charge that brings jail time with it," Writman stepped toward her and Eu didn't budge an inch.

"I'm not obstructing. I'm trying to figure out what happened."

Carter lifted a hand toward Writman, a silent gesture to get him to back off. "I understand. But he's not wrong," he explained politely. "We've been doing this kind of work for a long time, and we'll get to the bottom of it. You just need to sit tight and cooperate, which means staying away from any of the details of the case. If you see or hear anything that you think might be pertinent, let us know about it. We'll take care of everything else. Are we clear?" Carter said, his tone firm but still polite.

"Crystal," Eu replied. She glared at Writman one last time before they left her porch. He glared right back, then did the I'm-watching-you gesture by pointing to his eyes then hers.

She closed the door and leaned back against it, fuming.

"I'm going to solve this case just to prove these people wrong," Eu muttered through clenched teeth. "Forget the article for now. I'm going to dissect every detail I can find about Lexie and Nate Rouse."

Armed with her laptop and a dish with two of Michael's chocolate chip cookies on it, and a mug of coffee to wash them down, Eu sat back down on the couch and slipped into fearless reporter mode.

"I wonder if Lexie or Raz ended their affair," she mused.

She clicked on Lexie and Nate's wedding website and began reviewing video while munching on her cookies.

"What do we have here?" she said, stopping the video and running it back, then enlarging the image, peering closely at it.

In the background of one of the dance scenes, Benz and Raz were off to the side of the stage, having a very animated argument.

"I wonder what that was about."

Making a note, but gathering no additional information from the video, Eu went to the photo gallery. After viewing what seemed to be over a hundred photos and finding nothing of consequence, she was about to give up until she stumbled upon a shot of Raz kissing the bride's hand while the groom glared at him in the background.

"Well, imagine that. Hello motive."

She took a screen shot of the photo and put it in a file, then continued searching through the rest of the photos without seeing anything else interesting. She yawned and stretched, rolling her head from one side to the other as her neck crackled in protest.

Glancing up from her screen for the first time in hours, Eu realized the sun had already begun to set.

"Oh, yikes. If I'm going to survive the winter with any money in my account, I've got to get this article written," she mumbled.

Doubts flooded her mind.

Was she really being as irresponsible as everyone seemed to think she was? Was searching for clues about a mother who never bothered to send her a birthday card even worth it? She pushed the intrusive thoughts aside and dove back into her work. She could dissect her decision-making abilities tomorrow.

CHAPTER SEVEN

After finishing her article at one a.m, Eu fell fast asleep and apparently stayed in the same position all night, because she woke up with a crick in her neck. Rubbing her neck with one hand, she yawned and glanced out the window, shocked to see a light snow flurry.

"Wait a minute. It's barely fall. How in the world is it snowing?" she murmured sleepily, rising to go to the window. "It's so… magical," she breathed. "We definitely don't have this in L.A. and I'm definitely not going fishing this morning." She shivered at the thought.

Making coffee in her pajamas, while her cinnamon roll heated in the oven, Eu watched the snow falling, mesmerized and still a bit groggy from her deep sleep. She'd just poured her first cup when there was a knock at her door.

"Are you kidding me? I can't get a minute's peace. What can they possibly want now?" Eu grumbled.

She headed for her bedroom, barking out, "Hang on a sec," as she passed by the front door.

Back in her room, she yanked on yoga pants, a thick hoodie from Trixie, and her slippers, then stomped back down the hall to the door and yanked it open, her scathing glare already in place for Deputy Writman. Who was actually on her porch was a complete surprise.

"Oh, I'm sorry, I didn't mean to intrude," Sierra said, her eyes wide.

Eu laughed. "No worries. I'm actually glad to see you. I was thinking it might be someone else."

"Oh, good." Sierra seemed to wilt with relief. "Because you looked pretty fierce when you opened the door."

"Yeah, I had another visit yesterday from two deputies who are trying to take the easy way out and blame me for everything rather than putting in the work to hunt down the actual criminal. I'm getting really frustrated with it."

"I'm so sorry they're bothering you when there are clearly others with the motive to have done it. That's ridiculous." Sierra shook her head.

Eu didn't mention they hadn't remembered speaking to Sierra. Their incompetence was just a given at this point.

"Well, at least it wasn't them this time," Eu said, smiling. "Would you like to come in? I was just about to sit down with coffee and a cinnamon roll if you're interested."

"That sounds perfect. I haven't really been eating much these days and a cinnamon roll sounds fantastic."

Eu hung Sierra's coat in the coat closet, and they sat down in the dining room, taking in the stunning view while they ate.

"These are delicious, thank you," Sierra said, taking small bites of her cinnamon roll.

"You're welcome. I wish I could take the credit, but one of the other owners here made them before he went back home for the winter," Eu replied, before taking a long drink of coffee.

"Have you been coming here for a while?" Sierra asked. "It's unusual to find resort people still here at this time of year."

"This is my first time, actually. This cabin used to be my mother's. I'll be staying through the winter, most likely. I work from home right now and this is a nice peaceful place to get some things done," Eu replied, glad to have someone to talk to for a change. "Have you lived here your whole life?"

Sierra shook her head. "No. I moved here after I graduated from college. I don't really get along with my parents, and I wanted a more remote life, so I totally understand how you'd want to be here through the winter."

"If you wanted a more remote life, you probably don't live in a resort then," Eu said with a grin.

"Definitely not. I'm not the resort type, even though ones like this aren't snooty and pretentious," Sierra replied. "I can't deal with people in ivory towers looking down on everyone else."

Eu nodded. "I'm definitely not the snooty type." She hadn't thought Sierra seemed like a free-spirited hippie kind of person like Fran, but she didn't really know her that well yet.

"So, where are you from?" she asked, then popped a strip of cinnamon roll in her mouth.

Sierra shrugged. "All over, really. My dad was a corporate ladder climber type, so we moved every couple of years. It's really hard to make friends when you know you're just going to move away from them again. That was one of the things I really liked about Raz. He was born and raised here and didn't have any plans to move on. He had the stable background that I never had, I guess." Sierra's eyes clouded with tears, and she took a sip of her coffee. "So, what are you going to do about the deputies bugging you all the time?" she asked, changing the subject.

Eu's heart went out to her.

"Well, I think I'm going to look into things a bit myself so I can clear my name," she said.

"That's so amazing. I hope you do. It's frustrating waiting to find out what happened and why, you know?" Sierra said, blinking rapidly and taking another drink of coffee. "Thank you so much for inviting me in. I don't want to overstay my welcome, but when I went down to the fishing hole to find you and you weren't there, I was kind of worried, all things considered."

"Thank you, I appreciate that. Seems like everyone is concerned about my survival these days." Eu chuckled.

Sierra smiled, then blotted her mouth with a napkin and stood to go. Eu grabbed her coat from the foyer closet and opened the door.

"Thanks again for the cinnamon roll and coffee. It's nice having someone to talk to," Sierra said, standing on the porch.

"Same here," Eu replied. "Be careful out there, the roads are probably a little slick with these flurries."

Eu closed the door, her spirits lifted by good food and conversation. She cleaned up the dishes and settled in on the couch again to get some work done. When she opened her computer, she realized she hadn't looked into Murphy's husband at all yet, and wanting to leave no stone unturned, she rationalized that a quick search wouldn't hurt her productivity.

She found the listing for Murphy's wedding website easily enough, but when she clicked on it, she went to an error page that said the site no longer existed.

"That's odd," Eu mused. "I wonder if she took the site down because there was something about her or her husband in the photos or videos, or maybe even in the comments."

With all thoughts of her work pushed entirely from her mind, Eu navigated her search to Murphy's social media pages, where she discovered that Murphy is a social media influencer who records and sensationalizes nearly every aspect of her life for public display, and that she likes to have a complicated latte at a local coffee shop, Hillside Coffee Company, every day around two o'clock.

Eu glanced at the time and hurriedly clicked back over to her article to make sure that she finished her work in time to be at the coffee shop at two.

CHAPTER EIGHT

Eu became a fan of Hillside Coffee Company the moment she entered the rustic little shop and was enveloped in the aroma of freshly roasted coffee beans. The barista who took her order was pleasant and helpful, and her first sip of an indulgent latte she refused to feel guilty about was so lightly sweet and creamy that her eyes nearly rolled back in her head. The taste reminded her of an upscale spot in L.A, right next to the newspaper building, where she used to go at least twice a week to get a drink that would help her cope with her incompetent boss's foibles.

There were only a handful of customers in the shop, so Eu was able to get a seat in the far corner of the room, where she had a panoramic view of the interior, so she'd know the moment that Murphy walked in the door. Not that she could miss it, as it turned out.

Eu was sipping her latte and watching a slow flurry of tiny snowflakes drift by the window, when Murphy entered, speaking loudly into her phone, which was attached to the end of a selfie stick. She fluffed her highly processed hair and chomped her gum while she walked and talked to the camera, leaving Eu to wonder how she managed to not walk into walls.

Before reaching the counter to order, Murphy scanned the room, doing a double take and freezing in place when she spotted Eu. Her lips curled into a snarl, and she moved the phone closer to her mouth to record something that she said in a much lower voice before she marched over, still filming, and positioned herself in front of Eu's table at an angle where she could capture both herself and Eu on video. She wasted no time in getting to the point.

"You lied to me. The police told me about it. From what I heard, they're pretty tired of you poking your nose where it doesn't belong. I should sue you for misrepresenting yourself," Murphy threatened loudly, seeming to act angrier than she actually was.

Eu figured she was merely mugging for the camera in order to get more likes on her video, so she cocked her head and replied in a normal, conversational tone of voice.

"You know that's not a thing, right?"

Her simple statement seemed to actually infuriate Murphy. She looked like she wanted to stomp her foot and throw a tantrum.

"What's your deal anyway?" she sneered, turning slightly as she checked the camera angle. "Are you one of those creeps who watches the news to find murders so that you can go pretend to be Scooby Doo or something?"

Eu smiled slightly. "No, not even close," she replied in an amused tone, knowing full well that Murphy was baiting her. She could play the acting-for-the-camera game, too.

Murphy's eyes narrowed when she didn't get the reaction that she clearly wanted. "Look at you, just sitting there calmly smiling like a psycho. You're probably the one who killed that sad excuse for a DJ and you're just looking for someone else to blame. Is that what you're doing? Because that would be defamation, and I could sue you for that, too," she threatened.

Eu took a sip of her latte and set it down. "No, but since you seem to be just itching for a fight and are being way melodramatic so that you'll some extra likes on your video, I figure at least one of us should stay calm and clearly that has to be me. I'm just sitting here trying to enjoy my amazing coffee, shout out to Hillside, and at last count, you've threatened me with two bogus types of litigation. Is that how you like to spend your day? Kinda makes me feel sorry for you, actually."

"Don't you dare talk to me like that!" Murphy screeched. "You have no reason to feel sorry for me, you psycho. My life is amazing."

Eu gave her a patronizingly sympathetic look and calmly grabbed her mug to take a sip of her coffee. In a flash, Murphy leaned forward and smacked the bottom of the mug upward, dumping its contents all over the front of Eu's souvenir sweatshirt.

"Good thing it was starting to cool off. And it shouldn't stain since my hoodie is black," Eu said, blotting at her sweatshirt with a handful of napkins.

She gazed up at Murphy for a moment. "You know, if acting like a two-year old is what makes you happy, you must be over the moon right now."

Murphy exploded into a tirade and Eu sat back, pretending to listen attentively until she wound down. Her cashmere clad bosom heaved with what looked like indignation and she stared down at Eu, seeming to dare her to respond in kind.

Eu pursed her lips, pretending to consider her next words carefully before she delivered them. She felt sticky and chilled as the coffee soaked through to her skin, but she wasn't about to give Murphy the satisfaction of realizing that.

"Hmm. They say people with explosive tempers are more likely to be killers. Are you trying to accuse me of murder because what you really want to do is move the focus from yourself?" Eu asked sweetly. "You should maybe look in the mirror before hurling entirely unfounded accusations," she advised. "If you'll excuse me, I'm going to replace the amazing coffee you just wasted."

Eu stood up and when she tried to brush past Murphy, Murphy shoved her hard enough that she had to hold her arms out for balance to keep from falling. When she regained her balance, she turned back to Murphy, subtly glancing up at the phone to see if she was in the frame for the video shot.

"That's assault, you know," she said conversationally. "Do all of your followers know that? Hi, followers." She waved at the phone. "That might just be behavior that a killer would engage in. What do you guys think?" she asked, speaking directly at the phone.

"Don't you talk to them! This is a live feed and they're my followers; do you hear me?? Mine!" Murphy snarled as everyone in the coffee shop turned to stare. She tried to shut down the live feed, jabbing at her phone multiple times before her extra-long nails allowed her to hit the End icon.

Eu took that opportunity to head for the counter, where the barista lowered her voice and asked, "Wow, what's her problem? She's worse than usual."

"Who knows?" Eu shrugged. "But it looks like I'm going to need another latte. To go, please."

"Sure, no problem. It's on the house. Sorry you had to deal with that."

Eu gave her a reassuring smile. "No worries, I'll just come back during a different time of day next time."

Meanwhile, having clicked off her feed, Murphy turned to storm toward Eu and was headed off by a man wearing a badge on a lanyard that indicated he was the manager. Murphy tried to dodge around him and started arguing, but he calmly herded her toward the door and stood outside with his arms crossed until she climbed back into her oversized SUV and screeched out of the parking lot.

"Thanks again," Eu said to the barista, when she handed over an extra-large drink to go.

She met the manager just inside the door as she was on her way out.

"I'm so sorry. I don't tolerate that kind of behavior here. I can assure you it won't happen again," he apologized, digging a stack of coupons out of his vest pocket and handing them to her. "Please don't let this weird incident keep you away. I've never had anything like that happen in my entire career."

"No worries. Now that I've tasted the coffee, wild horses couldn't keep me away," Eu replied, raising her cup. "Thanks for the coupons."

"You're quite welcome. Have a great rest of the day."

Eu got into Michael's car and let out a sigh of frustration. "Well, that went well," she muttered as she drove away.

CHAPTER NINE

After taking a shower to wash off the latte that had soaked through her hoodie and bra, Eu tossed a load of laundry into the washer and decided to put the disastrous and very public encounter with Murphy behind her and get some work done. Tired of replaying the horrendous incident over and over in her mind, she was determined to be much smarter about her approach to investigating when she got back to it.

Thinking things through would probably be a good place to start, but for the next couple of hours she buckled down and got serious about getting a couple of articles knocked out. The murder investigation was important, but it didn't fill the refrigerator. She was so immersed in her research for the second article that she jumped when her phone rang. When Fran's picture popped up on her screen, Eu answered immediately.

"Everything okay?" she asked, wondering why Fran would be calling out of the blue during the middle of a work day.

"For me, yeah, everything's peachy," Fran replied. "For you? Uh… I'm not sure, actually."

Eu's stomach did a queasy flip-flop. "Oh, boy. What's going on?" she asked, bracing herself for her best friend's reply.

There was a moment of hesitation before Fran spoke again.

"Yikes. You haven't been on social media today, have you?" she asked.

Eu shuddered, wondering where she was going with that. "Other than doing some checking around on potential suspects, no. I'm not a huge fan of it, as you know. Why do you ask?"

Fran sighed heavily. "I hate to break it to you like this, but it seems you've gone viral and have become a bit of a social media celebrity," she replied.

Relieved, Eu laughed. "Ha-ha, very funny."

"Eu, listen to me. I'm not joking. I don't know what you did to make Murphy Miche hopping mad, but her live feed from some coffee shop where she attacked you went viral. Now her former followers are leaving her in droves and saying that you're some kind of hero for standing up to her."

Eu's heart dropped and she felt a bit faint. "Wait, what?" she whispered. "How do you know who Murphy Miche is?"

"Oh, honey, everyone knows who Murphy Miche is. She's everywhere on social media," Fran replied. "I went over and checked out some of your accounts, and people are posting all over your pages about how brave you were and how much they admire you," Fran replied.

"Yuck," Eu said, swallowing hard as her stomach clenched.

"Yeah, she's definitely not someone I'd want to tangle with and now that her followers are loving you, she's going to go ballistic. What the heck is going on out there, Eu? I know you said there was another murder, but what does that have to do with her?" Fran asked.

"Well, I think she's a good candidate for a suspect in the murder, so when I found out she had some bad blood with the victim, I kind of pretended to be a customer service rep from the victim's company to get some information out of her," Eu explained, feeling a blush rising hot in her cheeks. "I probably shouldn't have pretended to be someone I'm not."

"Yeah, I'm thinking that probably wasn't your brightest move, but I mean, sometimes in these bizarre situations you keep getting yourself into, the ends justify the means," Fran replied, blowing out a breath. "So, now what are you going to do?"

Eu closed her eyes tightly for a moment and shook her head. "I'm so out of my depth here. I have no earthly idea what I should do."

"You could go on social media and make a statement? Apologize, or say something that might make Murphy calm down a little?" Fran suggested.

Eu frowned. "That doesn't make sense, though. Why would I do that? Wouldn't it make me look guilty if I suddenly started acting nicely to her after she pulled that stunt? In public, no less?" she asked, remembering the shocked looks on the faces of the customers in the coffee shop.

"Murphy is all about her image. She's all style and no substance from what I've seen, so if you say something that might help mitigate some of the damage she did to her reputation, she'd have no choice but to be nice to you after a gesture like that. Normally, I'd say, no, you had every reason to make her look bad, but that kind of person makes a much better ally than enemy, and you can use all the allies you can get right about now," Fran explained.

Eu sighed. "I think it would be more of an armed truce, but yeah, I see what you're saying. I'm going to finish my article, have dinner so I can think straight, and then get online to see how bad things are looking on my social media pages. I'm not even going to try and decide how to handle it for a while, until I can focus and think about it."

"That makes sense," Fran replied quietly. "I'm worried about you."

Eu choked up a bit at her bestie's tone. "I know, but don't be. Don't worry. One way or another, I'll get through this. Thanks for letting me know. I may call later to vent."

"You know where I am, honey."

"I know. Love you, girl."

"Love you, too."

Eu hung up, and despite the fact that her stomach was in knots, she was suddenly ravenously hungry. Social media could wait for the moment. First things first. She needed food. She always thought better on a full stomach.

"I need both food and comfort, so it has to be pasta," she murmured, going to the freezer chest in the pantry and pulling out a bag of her homemade gnocchi.

She spent the next half hour making an impromptu tomato and herb sauce while sipping on a glass of pinot noir, and as soon as she tossed together the gnocchi and sauce and pulled fresh garlic bread out of the oven, she sat down to eat, not even attempting to think.

After devouring the delicious food, Eu glanced over and saw the battery light on her laptop blinking like a beacon, beckoning her to take action. It was time to go assess the damage and make a plan.

She cleaned up the kitchen, then went to the couch and opened her laptop.

"And now we see what going viral looks like." She sighed.

CHAPTER TEN

Scrolling through her normally neglected and sparse social media presence, Eu was both horrified and amazed to see the reaction her incident with Murphy had caused. There were kind messages of support for the way she'd handled the situation from tons of people, but there were hate bombs from some of Murphy's most loyal fans, too.

After wading through what seemed like hundreds of comments, without even scratching the surface of all the recent activity, Eu removed the numerous friend requests from Murphy's former followers. Her curiosity got the best of her, however, and she clicked on some of the profiles of those who had left hateful and often threatening messages.

Chilled by the level of negativity, Eu shivered, the hairs on the back of her neck rising. She'd just finished reading a particularly violent message when she noticed a light flickering outside, near the side of the cabin.

Thoroughly spooked, she tiptoed to the sliders in the living room that led to the deck and stood behind the drapes, peering into the darkness. Her heart racing, she spotted figures moving around in the darkness, and no matter how much she squinted, pressing her nose against the glass, she couldn't identify them. Until she heard a squawking sound. A law enforcement radio squawking sound.

Adrenaline screaming through her body and feeding her rage, Eu marched to the front door and looked out, seeing a police cruiser parked just beyond her parking spot in the lot. Without even bothering to grab a coat, she opened the door, and, using her phone as a flashlight, stomped down the path that led to her dock behind the house, where pairs of deputies appeared to be searching for something.

"Now what?" Eu called out in frustration, her voice echoing in the stillness of the evening.

"I'm going to have to ask you to stay away from this area for now, ma'am." A deputy moved up the path toward her, holding up his hand like a crossing guard.

"You must be kidding me. This is my cabin and that's my dock." She inclined her head toward the activity taking place behind the deputy. "Just what exactly is going on here?" Eu demanded, hands on hips, the light from her phone shining on her slipper-clad feet.

"We received a call from somebody thinking they saw something on the day of Raz Wiles's murder," the deputy replied.

"Well, that's wonderfully specific." Eu arched an eyebrow at him. "Who was it and what did they think they saw?"

Her nemesis, Deputy Writman strode up the path, approaching just in time to interrupt. "All due respect, you ain't getting no information about an ongoing investigation and if you keep trying to mess with it, you're gonna find yourself in jail. Am I being fairly clear?" He hitched up his gun belt and stared at her.

Everything about that set Eu's teeth on edge, but it seemed as though it would absolutely make Writman's day to take her to jail, so she had to bite back her automatic response. Just as she got a grip on her temper and opened her mouth to speak, someone down by the dock called out. "Found it!"

"Found what?" she wondered aloud, hoping hard it wasn't another body, as the other deputy and Writman scurried off toward the dock.

"Keep back. I mean it," Writman called back over his shoulder, following the other deputy down the path.

Eu stood shivering, watching the dancing flashlights skimming over the surface of the land and water near her dock, bathing the perfectly normal surfaces in a sickly glow. Suddenly, even with a contingent of law enforcement merely yards away, Eu realized just how alone and vulnerable she was out there in the darkness. With one last look toward the dock, she hurried inside, her heart in her throat.

She wrapped a silky faux fur blanket around herself, poured a glass of wine to help calm the quaking in her stomach, and stood in front of the slider, watching the activity near the dock. It appeared as though everyone's attention was focused on a small post near the water's edge that had her cabin number painted on it.

"What could they possibly be looking at?" She murmured, her breath making a thin veil of fog on the glass in front of her.

When two figures moved back up the path toward the cabin, Eu braced herself, expecting a knock on her door. She still jumped when it came. Sighing, she put her half-empty glass of wine on the counter and went to open the door.

It was Carter and Writman, of course. "May we come in?" Carter asked, his tone polite, but grim.

Eu sighed. "Is it really necessary?"

"We can get a warrant if you're not going to cooperate," Writman snapped.

"Fine, whatever," Eu replied, tired of the constant bickering with the irascible deputy.

"Do you mind if we take a look around?" Carter asked, once Eu had shut the door behind them.

"Be my guest. I have nothing to hide." She shrugged.

When the two deputies began systematically searching the cabin as though they might find something incriminating, Eu sat on the couch drinking her wine while pretending to be working.

She'd scrolled through the purse section of her favorite online shop almost entirely by the time Carter and Writman came back into the living room.

"Well, clearly you didn't find any bodies, or drugs, or whatever other outlandish things you happened to be searching for," she said dryly, setting her wine glass down on the coffee table.

"You might wanna watch that attitude, little lady," Writman said, scowling at her. "Things just got a whole lot worse for you. You wanna tell us the truth about what happened now?"

Eu's stomach churned. "I have no idea what you're talking about."

Writman glared at her and Carter stayed silent.

"Look here, y'all can play dumb all you want, but the piece of the victim's shirt and dried blood that we just found on the signpost by your docks speaks volumes. You'd best consider telling the truth sooner rather than later," Writman said, hooking his thumbs in his gun belt.

Eu's mouth went dry.

CHAPTER ELEVEN

Eu sat on the couch in her pajamas, staring out of the sliders and drinking strong bracing sips of coffee, still stunned and shaken that the deputies had found evidence linked to Raz Wiles' death so close to her dock.

Her phone, beside her on the cushion, dinged, signaling an incoming text. Eu picked it up with no small amount of dread but let out a breath of relief when she saw that it was Michael who had texted. Her pulse quickened when she saw his name on her screen.

"Hey, just checking in. Are you okay?" he wrote.

Eu's eyes filled with tears both at his kindness and at her situation.

"No. I'm not. The sheriff's deputies were here again last night. I'm really sick of being blamed for things that have nothing to do with me. It's not fair," Eu replied, wiping her tears with the back of her hand after she finished.

"Well, there's certainly no shame in packing up and leaving after this mess is all cleared up."

Michael's words leapt out at Eu from her phone screen. He hadn't meant it in a bad way, he was just trying to give her a way out. He'd, in a sense, given her permission to give up.

"But I'm not a quitter," Eu murmured, her former resolve rising to the surface.

"Heck no," she wrote back. "I'm going to prove my innocence and stay right where I am until I make the decision to move on, whether anyone else likes it or not."

"There she is. That's the Eu that I met. Strong, determined."

Eu blushed.

"You set me up for that reaction," she accused, putting a playful laughing emoji at the end of her sentence.

"Maybe, but I think sometimes it's perfectly okay to say something that will help a fellow human remember how awesome they are."

"Awesome? I don't know about that, but I am stubborn. My dad used to tell me that all the time."

"A dad would know, LOL. So, what's happening with the case? Any updates?"

Eu filled him in on the coffee shop incident with Murphy and told him how it had gone viral.

"Yikes. Sounds like you handled it well at least."

"Yes, but I think she probably set me up somehow because she hates me, and I can't figure out how she did it. It's awfully convenient that evidence showed up and police found it after an anonymous phone call that took place after the coffee shop debacle," Eu replied. "My next move is to talk to Nate Rouse."

"I'm worried about you. He's a dangerous guy, and I've generally found it better to walk away from a hissing snake than to go into its den and poke it with a stick," Michael warned.

"I get that, but at the same time, staying out of jail is worth the risk. I'm just a normal working girl from L.A. I've had no experience with the law or courts. I wouldn't have the foggiest idea how to survive being incarcerated, even if it was only in the local lockup."

"Yeah, I don't think it'd be a good environment for you. Please be careful, and don't hesitate to call if you need anything."

"I will. Thanks, Michael."

"Anytime."

Eu's phone was silent after that and while she missed having Michael to talk to, she'd somehow been inspired by their short chat to take action again, rather than wallowing in pity and fear.

She opened her laptop and was dismayed to see that she had tens of thousands of notifications from supporters, followers, and yes, haters.

"Fran was right. This is out of control; I have to do something about it. I have to put up a post that will make everyone calm down and forget that I exist," she mused. "Here goes nothing."

Hi everyone,

I just wanted to say that I'm really no one special. In fact, I probably should have just walked away when things started to escalate in the coffee shop. I always try to keep in mind that we never know what people might be going through.

If you've supported Murphy in the past, I hope that you'll consider supporting her again, because she may have just had a bad day, and shouldn't we all forgive each other when that happens?

I'm touched and flattered by your kind messages and follows, but I'd encourage you to see if you can be there for Murphy again. I'm boring by comparison, I can assure you.

Thanks, and I wish you all well! Eugenia

"There," she said, letting out a breath. "That was easy, and hopefully it's the end of all that nonsense. Now, it's time for a little meeting with Nate Rouse. Ready or not, here I come, Mr. Personality."

CHAPTER TWELVE

"Hi, I'm here to see Nate Rouse," Eu told the bored looking receptionist at the accounting firm.

Taking a page out of Murphy's bag of tricks, she had her cell phone in her shirt pocket, with the camera facing outward and the video feed turned on so she could record her interaction with Nate Rouse.

"Is he expecting you?" the young man asked, thumbing through a scheduling book. "I don't have any appointments booked for today."

"Oh, that's great," Eu said brightly, hoping to charm him into submission. "Then I can just steal a few minutes of his time and be on my way." She leaned in and lowered her voice, "I'm a customer service rep.

He made a complaint, so I have to follow up. It's not fun, but it's part of the job." Eu shrugged.

"Oh, that bites," the young man said, giving her a sympathetic look. "Down the hall, last door on the right. May the odds be ever in your favor," he said wryly.

Eu grinned. "Thanks."

Before she could change her mind after the receptionist's warning, she strode down the hall. Nate Rouse's door was open, so she knocked on the frame before entering. He frowned and raised an eyebrow in a distinctly icy manner.

"Are you lost?" he asked.

"Not if you're Nate Rouse," Eu said, using the same smile that had won over the bored receptionist.

He glanced at his watch and gave her a pointed look.

"I'll be brief." Eu stepped into the room and stood about three feet away from the front of his immaculate desk, edging toward the chair in front of her since he hadn't invited her to sit. There wasn't even a speck of dust on the pristine walnut desk. "I'm a customer service representative from Dream Makers Enterprises and…"

Nate Rouse shot to his feet, his face contorting in an angry grimace.

"Don't bother with your drivel. My wife warned me about you. I don't know what your game is, but you clearly don't know who you're messing with. Stay away from me and my wife, or I'll get a restraining order, and your social media fans won't think you're the good guy anymore. You don't want that. When those people turn on you, things can get ugly," he said, looming over her, eyes glittering like a snake that was about to bite.

"That sounds an awful lot like a threat, Nate Rouse," Eu articulated his name clearly for the recording.

"I don't make threats. Now get out of my office before I pick you up and throw you out." He took a step around the desks, his hands balled into fists at his sides.

"Wow, I thought people were exaggerating, but it turns out you really are as rude as they said you were. Have a great day, Nate."

Her heart pounding, Eu backed out of the office slowly, keeping an eye on the irate man in front of her. His face was tomato red and he had a vein pulsing in the center of his forehead.

Once she was out in the hall, she hurried toward the exit.

"He's a jerk," the receptionist whispered sympathetically as Eu breezed by his desk.

Eu widened her eyes and nodded in agreement, then took her phone out, hit the stop recording button and showed it to him. With a look of awe, he grinned and nodded.

"Nice," he said in a low voice.

Eu winked and went out the door.

Back in Michael's car, she sat for a few seconds, taking deep breaths in and slowly letting them out. There was no doubt in her mind that Nate Rouse could kill, probably with his bare hands, with sufficient motivation. If he found out that his wife had an affair with Raz shortly after they were married, that would definitely constitute sufficient motivation for someone like him with a hair-trigger temper.

Continuing to breathe deeply on her way back to the cabin and needing to take a step away from talking to potential murderers for a bit, Eu decided that, since it was a nice day, she'd take her laptop out to the deck and work on a few more articles, while getting some fresh air.

She'd been working away, while chain-drinking coffee, for about an hour when she heard the sound of a good-sized boat engine near her dock. Standing at the rail, she looked over and saw Benz Zoeller expertly pulling his boat up to the dock. She waved down and him and he waved back.

After stepping onto the dock, he trotted toward the cabin.

"Hey, there. How's it going?" he called up to her.

"Good. Hang on a second, I'll come down," Eu replied, closing her laptop and slipping her feet into her shoes.

"What brings you to my cove?" she asked with a smile, when she came around the side of the cabin and greeted him.

"Thought I'd come by and check on you now that you're an internet celebrity," he teased. "You did a really nice thing writing that last post. Everyone seemed to like it."

"Wait… What? Everyone?" Eu repeated, wondering how he'd seen it.

"Literally everyone. It's gone viral and people are asking you for more content."

So, he'd read the comments, too. Eu was kind of flattered, but she sighed.

"Yikes. I was hoping that it'd make them all leave me alone and go back to watch Murphy's ongoing drama fest."

"Seriously though, how are you holding up?" Benz asked.

"Things have been beyond weird, but I'll be fine as long as I can convince the cops that I'm not a killer."

"Yeah, those folks aren't always the brightest, but Carter seems like a nice enough guy. Have you met him?"

"Way too many times, yeah. He seems okay. His partner is…" Eu just shook her head rather than finishing her sentence.

"Yeah, those two are definitely a good cop/not so great cop combination," Benz agreed.

"There are a few people I'm checking out, but honestly, I have to wonder if Murphy did it and is playing games with people because she loves the drama," Eu said, thinking.

"Interesting theory. Why do you think it's her?" Benz asked, cocking his head to the side.

"Because right after the little coffee shop drama, an anonymous caller told the police there was evidence near my dock and police found it on the signpost down by the water."

Benz nodded, seeming suddenly uncomfortable. "Have you looked for yourself?" he asked.

Eu shook her head and wrapped her arms around her midsection. "No. I'm not sure what they found, or if I even want to know."

"Understandable," Benz replied.

Eu was quiet for a moment, and though the thought made her skin crawl, she had to know. "I'm going down there. I'm going to see if I see anything. I know where they focused on the signpost, so it shouldn't be too hard to find."

"Don't you think they've taken whatever they found?" Benz asked, his eyes darting toward the water.

"One way to find out," Eu said, striding toward the signpost.

"I don't think the deputies would approve of you poking around, though."

"It's my yard, my dock, and my signpost." Eu shrugged, squatting down beside the post. "I won't touch anything. I just want to see." She peered closely at the post.

"Ugh, there it is," she said, eyeing a clump of blue threads that had been caught on a splinter, and a smudge of blood below it, part of which had been clearly scraped away and was likely sitting in a police lab somewhere. "But that's odd..." she mused.

"What's odd?" Benz asked, standing back.

"In order to snag himself there, the victim would have had to run up from the water. I don't have a boat, so why would they suspect me?"

"Well, you've said it yourself, you're an outsider, and you own the property." Benz shrugged. "Also, their only other options are an influencer and a local accountant, which if the sheriff accused them and was wrong, could bring a lot of heat on the department," he pointed out.

"Is that how it works around here? The people with the most money and influence get a free pass?" Eu shook her head in disgust.

"Not always. But a local celebrity… Who knows?"

It didn't escape Eu's notice that Benz fit that description as well, and she shivered when she realized that he'd been acting strangely since he'd heard about the evidence. Could he be the killer?

"Well, I'm just spinning my wheels even trying to figure this mess out. I'll just let the police do their job and try not to worry about it."

"That's probably best. Well, now that I see you're safe and sound, I think I'll head out," Benz said, eyeing the dock and his boat beyond it.

"Thanks for dropping by," Eu said, shivering and hurrying toward the house.

"No problem," Benz said flatly, striding away in the opposite direction.

"He seemed to be pointing fingers at Murphy," Eu murmured, watching his boat pull away from the dock from her dining room window. "Is he just covering his own tracks or is Neanderthal Nate the culprit?" she wondered aloud. "I'll either find out or die trying."

CHAPTER THIRTEEN

Frustrated after another bad night of sleep, where every creak and groan made her eyes shoot open, Eu woke up grumpy. Convinced that fishing would help her shake off her crankiness, she took a full thermos of piping hot coffee down to the fishing hole after putting on layers of clothing to combat the air that had now become chilly enough that she could sometimes see her breath in the mornings, a phenomenon she'd never experienced before coming to the Ozarks.

"This is crazy," she muttered, her breath coming out in little white puffs as she spoke, on her way down to the fishing hole.

"Good morning, Callie," she called out, forcing every last drop of cheerfulness that she could muster into her voice.

Callie ignored her, of course. Feeling petty, Eu regretted the fact that she didn't have enough energy to drive the hermit across from her nuts with chatter and had to content herself with sipping her coffee in silence, while waiting for a bite.

Minutes ticked away, and soon, with every passing second, Eu became more uncomfortable. She'd downed the thermos of coffee so quickly that now she had to go to the bathroom, and unfortunately, the well-appointed fishing hole didn't have one.

She reeled in her line and leaned her pole against the railing, then hurried back up to her cabin for a brief stop. When she crested the hill and stepped into the parking lot, she saw Sierra coming around the side of her cabin. Sierra looked up, grinned, and waved.

"Hi," she greeted Eu, her nose red from the chill in the air. "I figured that you wouldn't be fishing this morning since it's so cold out, so when you didn't answer the doorbell, I went around back to see if you were working out on the deck," she explained. "Did you actually go fishing this morning?"

"Yep. I woke up in a bad mood, and I thought fishing would mellow me out a bit," Eu confessed. "Then I drank so much coffee that I had to come back up here for a bathroom break." She chuckled. "Come on in," she invited.

"Are you sure? If you're not feeling like having company, I totally understand," Sierra said.

"Maybe company is what I need," Eu replied, unlocking the front door and letting them in. "Make yourself at home and I'll be right back," she said, hurrying down the hall.

She washed her hands thoroughly after she was finished, enjoying the warmth of the water bringing her cold fingers back to life, and the glorious scent of her mandarin orange hand soap. When she headed to the kitchen, she saw Sierra standing in the dining room, admiring the view.

"How about coffee?" Eu offered, thinking she'd make decaf this time.

"That sounds great, thank you," Sierra said.

Eu set up the coffee and hit the Brew switch, then grabbed some chocolate chip cookies out of the freezer and put them in the microwave to defrost and heat.

"Those smell amazing," Sierra said, her eyes lighting up when Eu brought the plate of them to the table, along with two mugs of coffee that she'd managed to hold in one hand by gripping their handles.

"They are. I can't take the credit though. I have a friend who bakes." Eu smiled. She always thought of Michael whenever she ate something that he'd left for her.

"Must be nice. So how are you doing? Are the police leaving you alone, finally?" Sierra asked before biting into a cookie. "Oh, my gosh, the chocolate chips are all melted. This is amazing."

"Yeah, I love it when they're warm," Eu agreed. "The deputies haven't been leaving me alone. They had an anonymous call about some evidence and came out here and found it, which I find to be a little too convenient, and the evidence doesn't even make sense." Eu shook her head.

"Well, I hope for both of our sakes that this nightmare is over soon," Sierra said. "Do you have an idea as to who might have done it? Since you're looking into things, I mean."

Eu made a face. "It's really hard to tell when it could be any one of the three people that I'm looking into. They've all been acting like they could have done it. It's a weird collection of personalities, that's for sure. I mean, Murphy Miche, a bridezilla who complained about Raz, attacked me at a coffee shop, then Lexie, another bride…" Eu trailed off for a moment, not wanting to be the one to break the news that Raz had an affair with a client. "She's just a horse of a different color and a friend of Murphy's, and Lexie's husband has anger issues and didn't like the way Raz handled their reception."

"Yeah, so many people were so mean to him, when he always did his best," Sierra lamented. "But my money is on Benz Zoeller."

Eu shivered a bit, remembering the weird vibe she'd gotten from him the day before when he dropped by.

"Why do you say that?" she asked.

"He was just so jealous of Raz. I think he partially blames him for his divorce. Things were never the same between them after that." Sierra shrugged and stared sadly into her coffee mug.

Eu made a mental note to track down Benz's ex-wife and start formulating an excuse to talk to her. Munching on a cookie, she stared out at the lake.

"Eugenia. Hey! Eugenia… Are you okay?" Sierra's voice rose.

"I'm sorry, what did you say? I didn't sleep well last night. I must've been lost in thought," Eu replied.

"I just asked what your next move is going to be," Sierra said, smiling kindly.

"I have no idea. Somehow, it's never worked out well when I try to communicate with my fellow suspects." Eu smiled wryly.

"Maybe you should just lay low for a while and see if the police can find any leads. Your stress level must be through the roof."

Eu nodded. "Yeah, it definitely is, but it'll be even worse if the only leads they find keep pointing back to me. Would you like more coffee?"

"I'd love to, but I have a ton of errands to run today. Thanks for the cookies and conversation," Sierra said, standing to leave. "Your poor minnow is probably frozen solid. Kinda like you. Would you like to borrow a coat? I'd be happy to bring one over for you," she offered.

"That's really sweet, but I'll be okay. I'm going to go to the thrift store and pick one up, along with some other winter clothes. I don't think capris and hoodies are going to work for much longer."

Sierra smiled and agreed. "Thanks for being so nice to me," she said. "It really helps."

"What are friends for?" Eu said, touched when Sierra's eyes clouded with tears.

They said their goodbyes and Eu closed the door.

"Now, let's just see what's going on with Benz's ex-wife," Eu said, and headed back to her computer, all thoughts of her frozen minnow dangling from her line pushed from her mind.

CHAPTER FOURTEEN

Settled in on the couch with her laptop, it didn't take Eu very long to find Benz's ex-wife's name, Alessandra Creswell. When she typed the young woman's name into the search bar, most of the articles that came up were from various charity events and formal occasions where she was surrounded by only those who were clearly high-society folk.

Apparently, she came from a wealthy family and the places that she tended to frequent were either outside of the country or behind gated areas so filled with the rich and shameless that there was no way that Eu could ever hope to gain access to talk to her. She was every bit the country club and yacht club girl and it seemed that she'd found a husband even more wealthy than Benz after their divorce.

When Eu found Alessandra's address by checking through real estate records following the announcement of her most recent marriage, she grabbed her purse and Michael's keys and headed out the door before her courage ebbed.

She pulled up to the gates of Alessandra's tasteful French chateau and pressed the buzzer.

"Your name?" a disembodied voice inquired.

"I'm a friend of Raz Wiles. I'd like to speak with Alessandra for a moment, please," Eu replied, feeling odd talking to a speaker in front of someone's massive home.

There was a prolonged silence before the speaker crackled to life again. Eu's heart leapt to her throat as she waited to see if she'd be granted an audience.

"Move along please. If you don't vacate the area immediately, private security and law enforcement will be notified."

"Wow. Well, you have a nice day, too," Eu muttered, closing her window and moving on before she had to tangle with law enforcement yet again.

Not wanting to waste a trip, Eu decided to go to the thrift store since it was on her way back to the cabin. Content to lose herself in the simple pleasure of shopping, she managed to find a warm, fluffy coat that reached nearly to her knees, and two pairs of thick hand-knitted mittens. At least if she had to go ice fishing this winter, she wouldn't freeze to death.

When she stepped up onto her porch, she saw that someone had propped her fishing pole, with its stiff minnow still on the hook, up against the railing.

"Did Callie do this?" she wondered aloud, the thought making her smile. It looked like perhaps her campaign to defrost the dour fisherwoman's personality might be working after all. Eu hoped she was getting closer to breaking through Callie's ironclad defenses.

Buoyed by the thought, she decided to do a bit more work on her painting, relying on her memory to capture the colors of the autumn leaves and the golden light, because many of the leaves had fallen and the light was beginning to look weaker somehow.

When she retrieved the painting supplies from the hidden space in her closet, she picked up the painting of the little girl and her daddy to examine it more closely. The little girl in the painting had the same color hair that Eu had at that age, and she wore red satin ribbons in it, like Eu used to. The man in the painting has the same shoulders and posture that she remembered her dad having before the illness that ended his life ravaged his body, making it bent and frail.

"Is this us?" Eu whispered, a lump forming in her throat. "Did my mother paint us? How would she have even known what I look like?"

As she examined the painting, heart, pounding, tears welling in her eyes, her fingers brushed against something on the recessed underside of the thick frame. She turned the painting over and saw a little folded piece of paper tucked between the frame and the canvas. As a tear rolled down her cheek and plopped onto the knee of her yoga pants, she unfolded it and saw a poem, written in careful script.

A whisper of what might have been, mourning what will be.

A question. An aching. It's more than me.

Everything I could ever want, but nothing that I need.

Buying, spending, crying, sending. My soul can't help but bleed.

Gone today, gone forever. My loves, my life, my everything.

Eu reads the anguished words aloud, tears flowing freely as the prose touched a chord within her that she couldn't begin to understand.

"If you didn't want to leave, why did you" she whispered, her heart aching. "I don't understand. What is even happening?"

Eu stared at the painting, tracing the outline of the man and his daughter with her forefinger, wondering if she was reading too much into what was probably just a coincidental painting that had been inspired by random strangers.

Her phone dinged loudly in her pocket, startling her from her reverie, and when she pulled it out, she saw that a text from Fran had come in.

Get on social media and go to Murphy's feed.

"Oh, no. What now?" Eu sighed, wiping her eyes and setting the painting supplies back in place.

She went back to the living room and opened her laptop, navigating to Murphy's pages. Murphy was livestreaming and was having a complete meltdown. Standing in front of Lexie's house, Murphy cried and raged into the camera while pointing at Lexie's white picket fence where someone had spray painted the word 'murderer' in red.

Seeing the event as an opportunity to take a swing at Eu, Murphy blamed the vandalism on her and told her, via social media of course, that she's not going to get away with it. She railed on, saying that she could spot a fake apology from a mile away and that Eu wasn't fooling anybody.

Since the video feed was live, Eu could see the comments on it as they came in. People who had been fans of Murphy's were responding to her accusations with derision, and in a couple of cases, with threats against her.

"This is out of control," Eu murmured, horrified. "I have to respond and nip this nonsense in the bud."

She typed a comment that said, "Someone broke the law. It wasn't me, and while I appreciate your support, no one should be responding to the situation with threats."

Eu's new and still rapidly growing fan base replied with adoration for her sensibility and kindness, which only served to enrage Murphy further.

"Okay, so that didn't work." Eu sighed and closed the laptop, rubbing her temples and trying to think.

Yet another rather hostile knock sounded at her front door making her jump, and she sighed.

"Seriously? I don't have time for Deputy Dawg and his sidekick while people are making threats against Murphy."

She opened the door and was beyond surprised when she saw a visibly angry Benz Zoeller on her porch. She greeted him politely, feeling uncomfortable after his spontaneous visit the night before, but he didn't respond in kind.

"I know you went to see my ex-wife earlier, and I don't know or care why, but you crossed a line. It's offensive. You're trying to meddle in people's personal lives and if Murphy Miche is any example, you don't care who you hurt in the process. That won't play well around here. You're in a vulnerable position and you need as many friends as you can get, so I suggest you lay off on pretending to be one of the

Scooby Doo gang, and just let the police do their job." His tone was still at a reasonable level, but he somehow seemed menacing, a muscle in his cheek twitching.

Eu swallowed hard, scared but angry. She figured if Benz was the killer, she was about to sign her death warrant, but after everything she'd been dealing with over the past few weeks, she was determined to have her say.

"I'm sorry if you feel that trying to exonerate myself for a crime I didn't commit is offensive, but nothing you could possibly say is going to stop me from trying."

When she saw his hands clench and unclench at his sides, Eu tried to shut the door and he quickly slammed his foot into the space between the door and the frame, preventing her from closing it.

"Now you listen to me…" he growled.

Behind him, someone loudly cleared their throat, and he turned, removing his foot. Eu saw Callie standing there, a don't-mess-with-me look on her face.

"Just checking that you got your fishing pole," she said mildly, nodding at the pole, then turning her steady gaze to Benz, staring him down.

"Uh, yes, I saw it. Thank you so much," Eu replied, her heart thundering in her chest.

"You were just leaving, right?" Callie said, still staring at Benz.

Without a word, he glanced at Eu, then back at Callie, and headed to his car, giving Callie a wide berth.

"Thank you," Eu whispered, leaning heavily against the door frame as he drove away.

Callie merely met her gaze, then turned and left.

CHAPTER FIFTEEN

Shaken by the encounter with Benz, Eu closed the door and locked it. Taking deep breaths, she sank into the couch to try and wrap her head around everything that had been going on. In minutes, there was another knock on the door, but this time it didn't sound aggressive at all.

Eu closed her eyes for a moment. Had Benz come back to apologize? "I don't want to see him even if he did," she murmured, wrestling with the decision as to whether or not she wanted to open the door.

"It's broad daylight, and Callie had my back the last time," she said with a sigh, deciding to risk it.

Much to her surprise, it was a delivery driver holding a gift basket.

"Eugenia Barkley?" he asked, his accent sounding charmingly comical as he butchered the pronunciation of her name.

"Yep, that's me," she replied.

"Here you go then," he said, handing over the large basket. "Have a nice day."

"Thanks, you too," she replied, an automatic response.

Just a peek at the basket made her stomach churn with dread. Inside it were cookies shaped and frosted to look like knives, a glass skull of diablo hot sauce that looked like blood, a red velvet cake shaped like a coffin, and sugar candy in sharp broken shards that looked like a broken record. Swallowing her nausea, she plucked out the card that had been tucked into the woven handle of the basket. It didn't have any indication of where it had come from, but there was a message typed on it.

We don't know if you've killed a human, or if you're just a killer human, but we love Eu. Murphy is a fake, but you're the real deal. Your fans, Lotus and Delia.

"Okay, that's the last straw," Eu said, feeling sick. "I'm setting all of my social media accounts to private right now."

She threw the gift basket in the trash and grabbed her laptop. There were even more people following her now, thousands of them, so before she made her pages private, she thought it would be best to check her messages for clues. She was looking for ones specifically from anyone named Lotus or Delia, but as she scanned, she saw one from someone calling themselves Dark Angel that was beyond disturbing.

"What's really funny is that you didn't do it, yet somehow, you think you're safe..."

Eu's blood turned to ice. She took out her phone and snapped a photo of the comment in case it got deleted later, then clicked on a photo that looked dark and scary to go to Dark Angel's profile. The profile had been created on the date of Raz's death and Dark Angel hadn't made any posts. The hairs rising on the back of her neck and goosebumps appearing on her forearms, Eu copied the link to the profile and emailed it to Michael to see if he knew how to track it to the source. He popped up in her chat moments later.

Hey Eu, this is definitely unnerving. I have a couple of students who are taking my Physics 303 class just for the challenge. They're Computer Science majors who happened to be sophisticated hackers, so I'll run it by them and see what they can find out. In the meantime, I know you're smart and I know you're careful, so you'll be okay, but it might be best to lay low for a while.

Eu replied: Yeah, that's the second time I've heard that today, so I might just take that advice.

Oh? Who was the first one to say it? Fran?

No, Sierra. She was Raz's girlfriend. I met her when she came to see the spot where he was found. We've had coffee a couple of times.

You have a kind heart, Eu. Remember, be aware of your surroundings, keep your eyes and ears open and try to think first and feel second when dealing with people.

I will. On a more interesting note, I found a poem tucked away in a painting that my mother had hidden away.

That's amazing! Do you think that your mother wrote it?

I don't know, but whoever wrote it had beautiful handwriting and liked parchment paper.

Eu typed the poem into the chat box and sent it to Michael.

Sounds like it definitely could have been her.

I don't know why, but it really kind of hit me all in the feels, you know?

Understandable. I think you're really brave for embarking on a journey to find out more about her. Thank you for sharing the poem with me.

Thank YOU for listening to all of my weird issues, Eu replied.

Anytime. I have to run, but text me if you need to. Be safe.

Eu had just finished typing out her goodbye to Michael when her phone rang.

"Oh, it's Fran, thank goodness," she said, hitting the answer button.

"Hey. Are you sitting down?" Fran asked, bypassing a greeting when Eu answered.

"Oh, man. Yes, why?"

"I've been following the news stations and papers in your area since I left and well, something happened. Something horrifying."

"What?" Eu asked, her stomach filled with dread.

"Lexie Rouse has been murdered."

"That's crazy, someone had just painted murderer on her fence earlier, remember?" Eu said, swallowing against the nausea that rose in the back of her throat.

"Who do you think did it? Could the same person have painted the fence and killed Lexie?" Fran asked.

"They could have if it was her husband. She had an affair with Raz, her hot-tempered husband killed Raz first, then Lexie. It all makes sense," Eu said, feeling faint when she recalled just how angry Nate Rouse had looked when he loomed over her in his office.

"And he knows you suspect him," Fran said, her voice trembling.

"Yeah, he threw me out of his office," Eu replied.

"Do you think the police will believe you?" Fran asked.

"I wouldn't believe me just yet. I need more information. A hunch isn't enough to go on," Eu said, trying to remember if she'd locked the door after her delivery.

"Be careful, Eu," Fran whispered.

"I will."

CHAPTER SIXTEEN

Needing some air, Eu put on her new thrift shop coat and went out onto the deck to gaze out over the water. The view, instead of it soothing her soul the way it had since she'd arrived in the Ozarks, made her feel vulnerable and exposed. If she went to the far left side of the deck, she could peek around the end of the peninsula and see Benz's house across the lake.

The neighboring cabin owners had stashed away their patio furniture, decorative flags and lawn ornaments for the winter, leaving them looking buttoned up and ready to withstand a harsher reality. The colorful additions that made the resort look so cozy during the season were stored in sheds and closets where they'd wait for the arrival of spring. Eu didn't even know if she'd still be there in the spring, a thought that made her stomach ache.

After just a few minutes, with the tip of her nose growing cold, she turned to go inside and when she did, she saw a dark smudge on the doorframe of the slider that led into the house.

Frowning she went in and headed immediately for the kitchen, where she wetted a dishcloth, then went back out onto the deck and scrubbed the smudge off, wondering absently if it had been her mother who had kept the cabin so meticulously clean.

All these years, Eu had pictured her mother, faceless though she might have been, summoning servants to do her bidding and not lifting a finger. Now, with little clues that kept popping up, she wondered if Miranda Bellingham had been so much more than she'd imagined, or if she was just creating an idealized version in her mind.

Dispirited, Eu rinsed and squeezed out the cloth, draping it over the faucet to dry, then took off her coat and hung it up. From the confines of her closet she heard yet another rapping on her door.

"Geez… Can't I even have five minutes to catch my breath?" she muttered, turning off the closet light and heading for the foyer.

It wasn't at all surprising when she opened the door and discovered Carter and Writman on her doorstep yet again.

"How nice, it's my daily visit from you. Are you here to apologize now that you know Nate Rouse killed his wife and her lover?" Eu raised one eyebrow, inwardly wincing at her rudeness, but wholeheartedly believing that they deserved it for bugging her nonstop and treating her like a criminal.

They ignored her question, and Carter handed her a document.

"This is a search warrant. On the basis of another anonymous tip, we're going to take another look around," he said.

"Let me guess, the anonymous tip person called themselves Dark Angel," Eu said, taking a shot in the dark. She made a face and shook her head but took notice and checked her attitude when both of them stared at her, clearly surprised. "Wait…was it Dark Angel?" she asked. "Because that was just a guess based on a particularly nasty message that I got on social media by someone with that screen name."

"Can we see the message?" Carter asked.

Eu opened her phone and showed them the photo that she took of her computer screen.

"And why is it that you took a photo?" Writman asked, eyes narrowed.

Eu wasn't about to clue them in on the fact that she wanted to share it with Michael and his hacker students. "In case they deleted it later. It seemed important, so I wanted proof that it happened," she said, speaking to Writman as though he was a five-year-old, then turned to Carter, who was the only one in the duo worth talking to.

"Don't you find it interesting that they're calling you guys with anonymous tips to set me up, while at the same time telling me they know I didn't do it, but I'm not safe. Call me crazy, but I think that sounds pretty darn contradictory."

Carter and Writman paused and exchanged a look, but neither replied.

"We're going to take a look at your deck first," Carter said, after a beat.

Eu made a sweeping gesture toward the sliders. "Be my guest. You have a warrant, you can go wherever you want, although getting one wasn't at all necessary, since I let you in without one last time you were here. Believe me, I want you to gather all the information that you can so that maybe you'll finally see that I'm not the one you should be focusing your efforts on."

She wondered absently if they'd find the murder-themed gift basket in her trash, but she had the card that came with it in her pocket if they questioned it.

They went out to the deck and immediately checked the doorframe precisely where she'd cleaned the smudge. They frowned at the spot, and Eu couldn't help herself, she had to explain what had happened.

"I don't know why you're fixating on that particular spot, but I just cleaned a smudge from there," she said, shivering as the cooler air wafted into the cozy confines of the living room.

"What did you use to clean it?" Carter asked.

"Just water and a dishcloth, why?" Eu frowned.

Carter turned to Writman. "You check here; I'll check the cloth." He then turned back to Eu.

"Where is the dishcloth that you used?" he asked.

"It's in the sink." Eu frowned, puzzled.

Carter followed her into the kitchen, where she pointed out the cloth. He slipped on a rubber glove, picked it up by the corner and put it into an evidence bag, then headed back out to the deck, where Writman had sprayed something along the side of the doorframe.

"We've got a positive," Writman announced, shooting Eu a scathing look. "But test the cloth to be sure."

Carter sprayed something into the bag and spots on the cloth began to glow faintly.

"Whoa, that's weird. You said something about testing positive. Positive for what?" she asked, staring at the doorframe, which was glowing where she'd wiped off the smudges.

Carter turned an unreadable gaze to her. "Bloodstains," he replied.

Eu felt faint, her stomach churning. "What? Why on earth would there be bloodstains on my slider?" she asked, a tickle of terror growing in her midsection.

Writman stood, his knees popping as he did. "Well, now, that's what we'd like to know."

His manner made it much easier for Eu to stiffen her spine and respond with strength, when just seconds before, she'd been ready to dive into bed and pull the covers over her head.

"Oh, please. Do you not see what's happening right in front of you? I'm sorry, but I find it a little too convenient that your 'anonymous' Dark Angel admits I didn't do anything, threatens me, then sends you out here where you magically find evidence." Eu used her fingers to make air quotes, then rested her hands on her hips, staring at Writman defiantly.

"We're taking the dishcloth into evidence," Writman said. "Don't even think about leaving town. We have enough to extradite you if you run."

Eu's heart began to pound in her chest, but she'd be darned if she'd let him see her fear.

A fleeting look that appeared to indicate impatience with his partner flitted across Carter's face, but it was so quick that Eu wondered if she imagined it. His tone was much more even than Writman's had been when he spoke to her.

"We'll check all possible avenues to try and figure out who the anonymous caller is," he said, heading for the living room, his eyes darting back and forth as he scanned, floor to ceiling along the way.

"Yeah, they might make a good witness in court," Writman said with a smirk, before following Carter to the living room, but not checking the area quite as thoroughly.

It seemed that his mind was made up. Case closed; Eu was the bad guy. But she wasn't. Which meant that there was still a murderer out in the world. One who had already threatened her.

"Doesn't it bother you at all that someone was clearly in my house? They obviously planted the blood and fibers down at the post too, because I seriously doubt that the victim ran up onto the shore from the water or careened off the dock at a right angle to bump into the opposite side of it. And if you looked closely, the fibers that were stuck there were cut, not torn. Then the same person somehow must have planted the blood on the doorframe, and at this point, we don't even know whose blood it is. It could've been from fish guts for all we know. If I had done it, do you think that I would've drawn attention to it by letting you know I had just cleaned it?"

"That would be a convenient theory for you, now wouldn't it?" Writman drawled.

"We dusted the post for fingerprints and came up empty," Carter said. "Same story with the doorframe. Whatever fingerprints might've been there were likely eliminated when you cleaned up the bloodstains."

Eu nodded, feeling sick. Her home had been violated, and she didn't even know where to look for a killer. There were so many possibilities. Nate Rouse seemed to be the most obvious, but how would he know where she lived? Murphy knew, somehow, and so did Benz. Both were angry with her at the moment.

Benz had a boat and could easily have come in from the marina to plant the evidence on the signpost. He had seemed so nice at first, but his manner had turned ugly fast when he discovered that Eu had been to his ex-wife's house. Had his niceness all been an act? Eu had a sudden realization. The first time she'd met Benz; he'd docked his boat in the same area where Raz's body was found. Had he been scoping out areas on the lake to drop a body? Since he lived all the way across the lake, there really wasn't any good reason for him to dock at the resort, even though he'd said it was a good fishing spot. And if he hadn't wanted to do the deed himself, he also had enough money to pay someone else do his dirty work for him. Someone like Dark Angel…whoever that was.

Then again, Murphy had plenty of money as well, and seemed to love internet sensationalism, so she could easily be Dark Angel, or could have paid someone to set Eu up. Frustrated, she shook her head and wrapped her arms around her waist.

Carter went back toward the guest bedroom, while Writman wandered leisurely down the hall. Not knowing what to do while they violated her privacy, Eu went into the living room and sat on the couch.

"Well, well, well… Now here's a room you didn't tell us about," Writman's voice drifted out to her.

Eu shot to her feet as Carter came out of her room and joined Writman. He stood in front of the linen closet at the end of the hall, where he had pushed against an interior sidewall that gave way, revealing a secret space that Eu hadn't known existed. He was shining his flashlight inside.

"I had no idea that was there," Eu murmured, dying to see what was inside.

"Looks like a storage area," Carter observed. "We'll check it out, then we'll be on our way," he said, following Writman into the space that had been built between the side of the linen closet and the back of the guest bedroom walk-in closet.

"There's a safe in here. Do you have the combination?" Carter asked.

Eu shook her head. "No, I didn't even know the room existed, so I definitely don't know anything about a safe."

"We can always crack it," Writman said.

"I think we have all we need for now," Carter replied.

When they finally left, Eu checked to make sure that all of the doors and windows were locked, then sat down with a glass of wine, shaking like a leaf as the adrenaline that had been coursing through her system hit with full force. "Why is this happening to me?" she whispered.

Turning on the television just for background noise helped dispel the eerie feeling that had gripped the cozy cabin ever since the arrival of the haunting gift basket, and Eu slowly regained her composure.

Making a hot cup of tea and taking it to the ensuite bathroom, she ran steaming hot water in her jetted tub and eased into the bubbles, taking soothing sips from her tea as her aching shoulders and neck began to relax. She had turned the television in her bedroom on, choosing a favorite sit-com, so that she could at least try to forget how terribly alone she was.

CHAPTER SEVENTEEN

Eu snapped awake, wincing at the pounding in her head, and realized that her phone had been ringing. She saw Michael's number on her screen and picked up immediately, still feeling more than a bit groggy after a very restless night's sleep.

"Hey Michael," she said, her voice raspy in the pre-coffee hours of the morning. "Everything okay?"

"Yes and no. My students were able to trace the IP address for your Dark Angel and went through some cyber gymnastics to determine who it is," he announced.

His revelation came as no surprise. Eu had done quite a bit of thinking after the deputies had left and had figured it out herself. The student hackers merely confirmed her hypothesis.

"I should have known sooner, but now that I do, I just have to call the deputies and tell them, and this can finally be over." Eu sighed with relief.

"I'm so glad. I've been worried about you, particularly when the Dark Angel struck again. I haven't had nearly enough of your company yet," Michael replied, causing Eu to blush profoundly, feeling warm from head to toe.

"Likewise," she said, her pulse quickening.

Elated, Eu got dressed in her most presentable sweater, brushed her hair, and even put on a touch of makeup, because she knew once she made her phone call and the deputies took the killer into custody, they'd probably come knocking on her door, hopefully for the last time. Ever.

She hoped to get an apology after everything was said and done but definitely wasn't holding her breath. First, however, coffee and headache relief were in order. Her upcoming call to the sheriff's department was crucially important, and she wanted to be as clear as possible on the phone, hence the need for caffeination, food, and pain reliever.

Eu sat at the kitchen table, gazing out at the water while drinking coffee, nibbling at a cinnamon roll, and waiting for her headache meds to kick in, when she heard yet another knock at the door. She ignored it. She was more than sick and tired of people dropping by unannounced to ruin her day.

Now that she knew who the killer was, and that things would be over soon, she could relax a bit. At least until her headache started to subside. She was kicking herself, because she knew that she was only paying the price for drinking red wine on an empty stomach last night…after a major trauma that had dumped gallons of adrenaline into her system. It had created a toxic brew in her system and today she was all about detoxing.

The knock sounded again, and Eu ignored it again. Then, an odd thing happened. There was a scraping sound at the door, and a loud click that sounded like it was being unlocked. Heart in her throat, Eu stood and spun to face the foyer. The knob turned, and she thought she might faint.

The door opened slowly, and she found herself face to face with the Dark Angel.

Play it cool. Don't let them see you sweat.

"I don't remember giving you a key," Eu said, trying her best to sound unconcerned.

"You didn't. I have certain skills that eliminate the need for such simple tools."

Eu nodded, her head pounding again, despite the meds. She was trying mightily to not jump out of her own skin and start screaming bloody murder. Or bloody murderer, as it were.

"Interesting. I imagine that comes in handy from time to time," she said, maintaining her illusion of calm.

"It does indeed."

"Like when you're planting evidence to frame someone?" Eu's tone was coy, almost playful. She was proud of herself. If she was about to die, she could at least score a few points on her way out. What she really wanted to do was buy herself time to figure out how to extricate herself from her wretched situation.

A shrug. "You made it all too easy. Such a great conversationalist. I would say you should be more discerning about who you share information with, but it won't be an issue for you soon." A smile.

"What a relief," Eu said dryly. "And it's with whom you share information by the way. Just for future reference."

"Being the grammar police isn't exactly your smartest move right now, but you're right to be relieved. I've heard that annihilation can be the sweetest form of relief." A twitch.

Eu's throat went dry, and her stomach seemed to wrap around her backbone. "So, you've done this before."

"What do you think?" A raised brow.

Eu smiled, though she felt very much like throwing up, passing out, or crying. "I think that the deputies standing behind you will be very interested in hearing more of your fascinating story."

An eyeroll. "You're bluffing. Don't even try it."

"She's not bluffing," Carter growled from behind the killer, slapping them in handcuffs before they even knew what was happening.

CHAPTER EIGHTEEN

"I just feel so…betrayed," Eu said, talking to Fran on the phone. "And dumb." She sighed.

"Okay, first of all, you aren't dumb, you figured out the truth before the deputies did, but how did you finally put it all together? Tell me everything," Fran demanded.

"It was partly my fault. When I saw someone who seemed to be in such emotional pain, my heart went out to her. I opened up and trusted her when I shouldn't have. I never would have guessed that Sierra was a stone-cold killer."

"You realize that just because that was the case with a murderer, it doesn't have to be that way in your personal life, right?" Fran said pointedly. "You have to trust people sometimes."

"Yes, I get that. I just can't believe I literally told her that I'm at the fishing hole every morning, then caught her lurking around outside of my house and believed her when she gave me the lamest excuse possible. She intentionally injured Raz before she killed him, and planned to frame someone for it, so she kept a vial of blood and a piece of his shirt. The police found it in her apartment. She used some of the shirt and blood on the signpost when I was down at the fishing hole, then, when I invited her in for coffee a few days later and had to leave the room to go to the bathroom, she smeared more of the blood on my slider to really set me up. Apparently, Sierra knew all about his reputation with the ladies and it's a good thing she was stopped because after she killed Lexie, she was going after Murphy next."

"Wow, I guess once you make one kill, it's a slippery slope from there," Fran commented dryly.

"I guess so." Eu shuddered. "I could tell by the look in her eyes that she had come to the cabin to kill me."

"Good thing the deputies showed up when they did."

"Yeah. Michael contacted them. He just had a sense that she'd be looking to strike sooner rather than later, so he gave them the information that his students had discovered and asked them to come do a wellness check on me. If he hadn't done that…I probably wouldn't be talking to you right now. Or ever again, actually." Eu blinked rapidly, her eyes welling in gratitude.

"Sounds like a big thank you hug and kiss is appropriate for that gorgeous professor," Fran teased.

"No, that's not at all appropriate. I mean, I wouldn't mind, but it's definitely not appropriate." Eu chuckled, wiping her eyes and blushing. "I did thank him profusely though."

"Have you told him how you feel about him?"

"Are you crazy? Of course not. I told you, he wouldn't be interested in me anyway."

"You might be surprised."

"I highly doubt…" Eu began, only to be interrupted by yet another knock at the door. "Hey, I'll call you later, someone is at the door," she told Fran, hanging up.

"Well, it's nice to know that at least I don't have to be afraid to answer it anymore," she muttered, hurrying to the door. She opened it and gasped.

"What are you doing here?" she blurted, eyes wide.

"I thought you might need a hug, and Callie isn't the demonstrative type," Michael said, with an adorable grin.

"You couldn't be more right," Eu agreed, launching herself into his arms and fighting back tears. "You saved my life. Thank you so much, Michael."

"It's a life well worth saving and you're most welcome. I'm going to be in town for a couple of days and I thought we could have dinner if you're up for it."

Eu tilted her head and gazed up with him, aware of the goofy grin on her face, but entirely unable to hide it. "Dinner sounds perfect."

CHAPTER NINETEEN

After a wonderful meal at the last restaurant in town that happened to be open for a few days longer, Eu, warmed from head to toe by good food, wine, and another hug from Michael when he walked her to her door, decided to venture into the secret room in the linen closet.

Sure enough, there was a small black safe built into the studs of the back wall of the tiny room. She tried the mystery key that she had found in the lock, but it didn't fit. On a hunch, knowing that she was likely going to be very disappointed when her hunch didn't play out, she turned the mechanical dials on the top of the safe to a set of numbers that she knew quite well – her birthday.

Click Click

Click Click

Click Click

Taking a deep breath, she pushed down on the door lever, and with a loud clunk that made her jump, it gave way. The first item that she saw in the safe took her breath away. It was a photo, sitting next to a wooden box. A very young version of her dad proudly had his arm around a beaming young woman who could only have been her mother. The image was nearly identical to what Eu saw every time she looked in the mirror.

"Mom," she whispered, tears falling.

She turned the photo over and saw a date, written in the same beautiful penmanship as the poem. It was just over a year before she was born.

Overcome, she held it to her chest, tears falling freely.

"I don't understand. If you were so happy, why did you leave? Was it because of me?"

Wiping her face, Eu carefully set the photo aside and pulled out the box. Inside was a pile of photos. Each and every one of them was of Eu. Every school photo, every birthday party and holiday. Every special moment in Eu's life had been tucked away in the simple wooden box.

Baffled, Eu saw an envelope in the bottom of the box. In the envelope was a sheet of parchment paper that had a cryptic message in her mother's handwriting on it.

You've taken all I have. There's no more to give. Now you've violated the only serenity I have left. My happy place. Wasn't it enough to break me? Did you have to destroy me as well?

Eu hung her head, her heart aching. "Have I been wrong about you all these years? Did you miss me, or even… love me?"

She wiped her eyes and straightened her shoulders. You can be darn sure that I'm going to find out.

***

If you enjoyed Casting Doubt, check out Baited Breath, book 3 in the Fish Camp Cozy Mystery series.

ALSO BY SUMMER PRESCOTT

Check out all the books in Summer Prescott's catalog!

Summer Prescott Book Catalog

AUTHOR'S NOTE

I'd love to hear your thoughts on my books, the storylines, and anything else that you'd like to comment on—reader feedback is very important to me. My contact information, along with some other helpful links, is listed on the next page. If you'd like to be on my list of "folks to contact" with updates, release and sales notifications, etc.… just shoot me an email and let me know. Thanks for reading!

Also…

… if you're looking for more great reads, Summer Prescott Books publishes several popular series by outstanding Cozy Mystery authors.

CONTACT SUMMER PRESCOTT BOOKS PUBLISHING

Twitter: @summerprescott1

Bookbub: https://www.bookbub.com/authors/summer-prescott

Blog and Book Catalog: http://summerprescottbooks.com

Email: summer.prescott.cozies@gmail.com

YouTube: https://www.youtube.com/channel/UCngKNUkDdWuQ5k7-Vkfrp6A

And…be sure to check out the Summer Prescott Cozy Mysteries fan page and Summer Prescott Books Publishing Page on Facebook – let's be friends!

CONTACT SUMMER PRESCOTT BOOKS PUBLISHING

To download a free book, and sign up for our fun and exciting newsletter, which will give you opportunities to win prizes and swag, enter contests, and be the first to know about New Releases, click here: http://summerprescottbooks.com

Printed in Great Britain
by Amazon